CONSUME ME

ALSO BY GENEVA LEE

THE RIVALS SAGA

Blacklist

Backlash

Bombshell

THE ROYALS SAGA
(IN READING ORDER)

Command Me

Conquer Me

Crown Me

Crave Me

Covet Me

Capture Me

Complete Me

Cross Me

Claim Me

Consume Me

Breathe Me

Break Me

GENEVA LEE

CONSUME ME

THE ROYALS SAGA: TEN

ESTATE
PUBLISHING + ENTERTAINMENT

To Ceej,
Thank you for being a light. You will be missed.

CHAPTER 1

ALEXANDER

No one had slept. There wasn't a chance in hell any of us would. Not tonight. Not until we found her. My inner circle had widened considerably in the last few months, but that wasn't what felt off now. There was a time when only Norris and Brex would have been with me during a crisis. Tonight, neither of them were here. In their place were questions I couldn't answer. I trusted my new allies, but that didn't make the others' absence easier to bear —especially since one of them was the last person seen with Clara.

"Again," I repeated, growing tired of my own question. There had to be something we were missing, some clue as to what happened in the time between the heart attack and my discovery of Clara's absence.

Sarah swallowed, looking around the room for a saviour, but no one spoke up. She'd changed into a loose pair of pants and a sweater that didn't match. Her dark hair was still curled elegantly from the evening's party and her make-up was tear-stained. "Norris and Clara took me outside. Norris called a car. It drove around and Norris helped me inside. The driver left a minute or two later without them and brought me here." She hesitated, her teeth sinking into her lower lip as her eyes filled with tears. "I'm sorry, Alex. I thought they were staying behind or...I didn't really think. I was...was..."

"It's okay," Edward said wearily as he tried to scrounge up sympathy. I heard the frustration running like a current in his voice. He hadn't bothered to change. There'd been no time between leaving the hospital and getting my call to come here immediately. He'd lost his tuxedo jacket and tie somewhere along the way. His husband was still fully dressed next to him, looking shell-shocked. "You were upset. No one blames you."

But I did blame her, which was why I didn't speak now. How could she not have noticed what happened to them? Why had Norris put her in the car first? None of it made any sense. The pieces didn't fit together to form a clear picture—the pieces didn't match at all. "Why didn't you ask the driver where they were?"

"I didn't think!" She hung her head, the tears spilling down her cheeks as she cried silently. "I just assumed they were coming in a different car, or they went back in, or..."

Across from her, Belle forced a sympathetic smile. My wife's best friend hadn't spoken a word since she'd arrived with her husband an hour ago. But where Belle appeared numb and half present, Smith listened to every word. I could almost see him filing them away for later analysis.

But what would he discover that I didn't already know?

Sarah had told us what she remembered, and it took effort to bite back more accusatory questions. Her story hadn't changed once since I'd woken her up a few hours ago. She'd been fast asleep on a couch in the Belgium Suite, still in her dress from the night's ruined party. The relief I'd felt when I'd found her was short-lived. She was alone, and her explanation of how she'd gotten home didn't make sense. Not because she wasn't being clear. I believed that she was self-absorbed enough to not care that she'd left the others behind. What didn't make sense was the breach in protocol.

What didn't make sense, quite simply, was Norris.

He wouldn't have sent Sarah home with a driver when I asked him to take her home. He wouldn't have put my wife in a different car. But the things that he wouldn't do— the things that had already been done—paled in comparison when I considered the things he would do.

He would protect my wife as if she were his own.

He would see her safely home if I asked him.

He would answer his phone.

I couldn't bring myself to consider why he hadn't done any of these things or why, even now, hours later, I couldn't reach him. Perhaps, because I couldn't face the only explanation that fit with what I knew of my best friend and most trusted advisor.

There was only one thing that would have prevented him from doing so, and it was a possibility I couldn't bring myself to consider, especially while Clara was missing.

A figure appeared in the doorway and I glanced up to find Georgia surveying the scene with careful eyes. With

Norris unaccounted for and Brex gone, she'd stepped into the role one of them normally occupied without batting an eyelash. I would be grateful if I wasn't angry at her, too.

"The sweep is complete," she said with the air of someone tiptoeing through landmines. There was a split second of hesitation before she told me what I already knew. "Neither Norris or Clara are on the grounds. We reviewed the security footage and they never came through the gates. We're trying to locate the driver that brought Sarah home."

I heard the unspoken *but* that should have accompanied that sentence.

"But we won't," I said when she didn't. "Was he on the footage?"

"I've called in some favors with MI-5. He was careful with how he drove." The statement was simple enough, but it was laced with meaning. She seemed to understand—as I did—the delicate situation we'd found ourselves in. Without more information, we might make the others panic if we dissected this revelation in front of them. Then there was the other consideration.

We trusted all the people in this room. That didn't mean we should.

"I don't understand," Edward burst out. "Where would she be? Where's Norris? Do you think she left? I know that you two talked about that."

My heart flatlined at his words, surprised that she'd shared that with him. Mostly because after the fight in which I'd asked her to move out—to protect herself and the children from me—she'd refused to even consider it. "She told you that?"

"She tells me a lot of things," he said softly. "She told me she wouldn't go." His voice broke on the words, the truth catching in his throat.

At this moment, we all wished it was as simple as her leaving me. We all wished she had because we knew one thing with certainty: Clara wouldn't go.

As each minute passed without word from her or Norris, it became increasingly clear that there would be no innocent explanation for what was happening. We weren't going to discover that she'd asked to go for a drive or had retreated to the country or gotten in an accident. Each moment not knowing erased one more possibility and took us closer to the nightmare I couldn't bring myself to face.

"Is there tracking at all?" Smith said stiffly, glancing between Georgia and me.

"It wasn't our car that brought Sarah here," I said. "We have to assume..." I couldn't bring myself to say it. I couldn't bring myself to admit what my brain knew but my heart couldn't accept.

"Not on the cars," he clarified.

Belle, who'd been gazing into the fire, turned to stare at him. Her mouth fell open in horror as she processed what he was asking. "Tracking her?"

"No," I said coldly. Even I wasn't possessive enough to implant my wife with a tracking device. I tried to ignore the small part of me that wished I had when he suggested it a few weeks ago. "There is no way to track her."

Not like that.

A sob spilled from Sarah, and she drew her knees up, hugging them. "This is all my fault."

A good man might have comforted his sister, but I didn't have time to deal with her emotional outbursts. Breaking down wasn't going to get us anywhere. We needed a plan. We needed to consider all the possibilities. Tears and self-recrimination were obstacles we couldn't afford. "You should go to bed."

She wiped her face, shaking her head. "I should stay. Maybe I'll remember something."

I doubted that and from the looks on the others' faces, they did as well. David put an arm around her shoulder. "Come on. I'll take you back to your rooms."

Sarah allowed him to help her up, but she stopped at the door. "Alex, can I stay in my old room—just tonight?"

Her fear splintered through me, creating a small crack in the determined veneer I clung to. Everyone was acting like we were planning funerals, not discussing strategy. I pushed it aside and nodded. "Of course."

Before they were out the door, a familiar form met them. Brex paused with a grim expression, tipping his head in greeting as they passed. But when they were gone, he didn't enter. Instead, he hung back, waiting for an invitation to cross the threshold into my private study. We stared at one another for a long moment. The usual smile was absent from his face and his eyes were shards of black coal.

"I called him," Georgia explained. "We're going to need his help."

She'd called, and he'd come. I'd considered doing the same, but I held no delusions he would come when I called.

But for her? Brex would come if Georgia asked, and I found myself glad that she had.

"My security credentials are still good," he said. There was a question hidden in his words.

I trusted Brex. I'd hoped he would come back. I hadn't expected it to be under these circumstances. "I'm glad you're here."

It wasn't enough. Someday we needed to talk about why he'd left in the first place. I needed to explain why I'd kept my prior relationship with Georgia a secret. I needed to apologise. But true friends always showed up when needed no matter how much you hurt them.

Brex joined us in the office, refusing a seat in favour of leaning against the wall. Georgia took Sarah's recently abandoned chair and drew a deep breath. Then to my surprise, she looked from Edward to Belle.

"We need to tell him. He needs to know," she said, her voice low but firm. Belle's mouth opened, but she didn't speak as she looked imploringly at Georgia. Edward's head dropped into his hands before he glanced up to meet their shared gaze.

I had no idea what these three could possibly need to tell me, but a chill ran up my spine like an icy finger. I waited for them to talk, dreading whatever was coming more with each passing second. Georgia was Clara's body-guard. Edward and Belle were her best friends. Clara shared a different relationship with them than with me. They shopped together and gossiped, and I'd never felt jealous of any of them until this moment. I fancied that my wife told me everything important. I'd never had reason to suspect otherwise until now.

"Tell me what?" I forced the question past my lips. A million possibilities tumbled through my mind. Perhaps I'd been wrong. Maybe she did intend to leave me. Is that why my brother had brought it up? Was there someone else? That possibility was laughable, but as the quiet strain between them continued, I was forced to realise that maybe I didn't know my wife as well as I thought.

Georgia peered at Belle expectantly. "Tell him."

"Me?" Belle's hand reached for her husband's and found it.

Jealousy crashed through me. She had someone to comfort her now as she faced something she didn't want to confront. The first numb wave of panic replaced the blistering sensation as I realised that she knew something that Clara hadn't told me.

"You know more than I do," Georgia pressed, "and he needs to know as much as we can tell him."

Belle's eyes closed briefly and I recognised the gesture. She was drawing from some well deep inside her—a place that it seemed all women hid inside themselves—for strength. I'd seen Clara do the same on a number of occasions. Every time it had been right before she'd delivered words I didn't want to hear.

I took a step toward the desk, gripping its edge to keep me upright.

"It's about the baby," Belle began and my fingers clutched the wood tighter. She seemed to notice and faltered. Her own knuckles had gone white as she held onto Smith.

"What about the baby?" I had to remind myself to breathe as I waited for her answer.

"There's something wrong with the baby's heart," Edward said when it was obvious she couldn't.

"What do you mean?" My words were strangled, hitching and hiccuping from me as I tried to process what they were saying.

Now that Edward had delivered the bomb, Belle seemed able to confess. "There's a problem with a ventricle. The baby is going...going to need surgery after it's born. Clara didn't want to worry you. She thought you might..."

The rest of her words faded even though her lips continued to move. The baby's heart. Clara had kept me from the doctor's appointments on purpose, because of the baby's heart.

"Alexander?" Georgia prompted when I didn't speak.

I shook my head, wanting them to continue. It took effort to focus on what they were saying when inside I was reeling.

"She's seen a few specialists. They advised her to keep her stress levels low." Belle was crying, but I couldn't find an ounce of sympathy for her suffering.

I couldn't find an ounce of anything. There was only one sensation unfolding in my chest. Shame. She'd been advised? How long had she known? How much stress had I placed on her in that time? Why had she allowed me to dominate her if she'd known? Was that why she'd sought release with me? I thought of the moment after the press conference. I'd told her to leave. I'd told her it was over. I could see her now, breaking on the floor and struggling to breathe as she begged me to make her feel something else.

She'd known then.

I had no doubt of that. I could see it now in my memory of that moment—one that I'd never be able to erase from my mind. It was etched like a tattoo on my soul. I'd tried so hard to give her up—and if I had...

Would she be safe now? Would the baby have suffered? Was there any decision that wouldn't destroy us?

"What happens?" I murmured, unable to find the strength to interrupt her entirely, but Belle heard. "What happens to the baby if...?"

I couldn't say it. I couldn't face it. I couldn't admit what I already knew.

What happens to the baby if we can't find them in time?

Clara's friends—her true confidants—shared a look that said enough. Then Belle whispered the words that broke me.

"I'm so sorry."

CHAPTER 2

CLARA

She was gone. One look and she'd fled like a frightened mouse back to whatever hole she'd crawled out of—but that didn't explain her ghostly appearance. For a moment, I'd mistaken her for someone else. Then I'd stepped closer and realized my mistake.

It wasn't Sarah, which meant Alexander's sister was somewhere else. Had she escaped? What chance did she have after…?

I shut my mind to the image of Norris's face, blood pouring from his mouth, but my stomach heaved. Too late.

Maybe my imagination was playing tricks on me. Maybe I'd hallucinated the girl. I had to be in shock or whatever they'd given me had side effects. I rubbed my belly protectively and felt a reassuring kick. If the baby was okay that was all that mattered.

For now.

But how long would that be the case? I didn't know where I was or why I was here.

The room was warm, even if it was about as welcoming as a prison cell. I didn't want to leave it to chase after what might have been a figment of my imagination. But she was the first sign of life I'd seen, which meant I didn't have a choice. Not if I was going to get us safely out of here.

The corridor stretched before me as silent and empty as it was a few minutes ago. The echo of my bare feet hitting the cold cement made me cringe. Could they hear that? Whoever it was that had brought me here? I scanned for cameras as I went but didn't see any.

No matter how hard I tried I couldn't put all the pieces together. Who was she? Why was she here? Why was I here?

Dread churned inside me, twisting and rolling in my gut until I thought I might be sick again. I fought the nausea. I couldn't afford to lose more fluids.

There was one spot of hope in this nightmare: I hadn't wound up here by mistake. I'd been taken.

It was an odd thing to find comfort in but surely it meant that someone would come. Eventually. And when they did, I would get answers. I would demand them.

And then I'd plead for my child's life.

It was a sobering thought. I spent the last few months preparing to fight for this baby—to make certain he or she lived. I never imagined it could come to this.

I trailed my hand along the wall, looking for something I missed, but the cinder blocks gave nothing away. There were no secret passages or hidden exits. The only doors were the ones staring back at me from either side of the hall

—the ones that were locked. Ones that led to unknown places.

There was also no sign of the ghost girl. It must have been me seeing things. Given everything that happened tonight—if it still was tonight—I couldn't trust myself.

Thinking back, I walked myself through the evening. We'd gone to the birthday party. Alexander and I had snuck off and made love in the museum. My thoughts drifted to the feel of his teeth on my flesh. Instinctively, my fingers skimmed over my breasts feeling the tender spots where he marked me.

It was real—that memory. Part of me wanted to retreat to it—to that last moment where I'd been in his arms, safe and protected. But the bite marks reminded me of something else: I was stronger than anyone knew.

Alexander had shown me that.

Someone thought they would break me. That was their first mistake. I expected them to make more.

I didn't want to leave that memory, but the answers didn't lie there. Still, I allowed myself a second to linger on the memory of his skin on mine. I could still feel him between my legs. Inside, part of me cracked, threatening to spill free. How much time had passed since those moments? Was he looking for me now? I sent a silent wish to him.

I wished he knew I was alive. I wished he knew I would find my way back to him. I wished he felt my love in that moment.

Pushing past the ache that threatened to overwhelm

me, I recalled returning to the party. I'd danced with Anders.

No, that had happened before Alexander had whisked me away.

We'd returned to the party in time for the cake. My stomach flipped again and the baby kicked as though put out by my rollercoaster of emotions. Mary.

She'd had a heart attack or stroke.

Why was everything so fuzzy the closer I got to this moment?

The memory plucked at me, but not because of this evening. I recalled being hurried out of the Child Watch Symposium. That day, Alexander had been waiting for me. What would have happened if he'd been waiting for me tonight?

But he couldn't have been. He'd been occupied with his grandmother. He'd gone with her to the hospital. Norris had seen to me.

I covered my mouth and sank against the wall.

Our guard was down because we were all focused on Mary. We'd been distracted.

The Child Watch attack hadn't been a miracle where no one got hurt. It had been a test run where they'd learned the two most important facts of my public life: Alexander would always come for me and Norris would protect me with his life.

And then they'd removed both obstacles.

Alexander was safe. He'd gone to the hospital. I couldn't bring myself to think about what they'd done to Norris, our best friend and constant companion.

If they were capable of that, what else could they be capable of?

I needed to find that girl.

I hadn't imagined her. I wasn't going crazy. Yes, I'd been drugged and brought here, but I was firing on all cylinders now. She was flesh and bone—and the only hope I'd had yet of getting answers.

So far, I'd been walking along, waiting for her to come out as I relived the events that had led me here. Now, renewed purpose drove me. I rushed to the first door and tried the knob. It didn't budge.

Neither did the second.

Neither did the third.

None of them.

Even the room I'd woken up in was now closed and locked. There was only one room to go to, but there were no answers there. Only a torn up book and a dresser filled with clothes meant for someone else:

The ghost girl.

I didn't know what else to call her. Was she behind one of these doors? Why had she come to me? That had to be her room. She must have seen me or heard who brought me in. All of that meant she might have answers.

The fact that she was behind one of these locked doors meant she might not be an ally, though.

Panic rose inside me and the baby began to squirm, reacting to whatever cocktail of hormones my anxiety was producing.

"Calm down," I ordered myself. Alexander would be

looking for me by now. Sarah saw what happened. Unless, she was here.

Unless she was with Norris...

Worrying about that—about her safety—wasn't going to get me closer to figuring out where I was.

I had two things I needed to do: keep calm and find that girl.

The baby's heart condition had to come first, but it wasn't easy to be zen when I was locked away god knows where. It's what I had to do, though, for both our sakes.

I pounded on the now-locked door I had awoken in. I was done walking around in a daze. I was done waiting for a door to open. I was done.

"Hello?" I yelled. "What kind of cowardly dickheads won't show themselves? Is this some kind of joke?"

It wasn't. At least, not the type that ended with finding out your friends were secretly filming you the whole time. I wished it was. I wished that a door would open and my best friends would step out, laughing, and proclaim this the world's worst gag.

No, this wasn't a joke. Once life and death were at stake, there was nothing to laugh about. I'd been here before. I'd faced death head on and I'd do it again now.

"My husband is coming for you!" I was screaming and my anger bounced back at me, fueling my rage. He would come. I knew that. The baby kicked hard as if seconding this opinion. He or she was defiant, too.

Good, the baby needed to be a fighter.

He was due in a few weeks and by then he would need all the stubborn tenacity of his mother and his father.

When he underwent surgery.

Which couldn't happen here.

The realization crashed through me. I wasn't racing against the clock. I was racing to defuse a bomb. The baby wasn't supposed to come yet, but if he did, what would happen?

There would be no one to help either of us. There would be no life-saving surgery. There would be no hope.

That's what I was searching for: hope. I'd take anything. A scrap. A crumb.

But the longer I looked and found the same bedroom waiting for me, the harder it was to keep the panic locked down. I didn't know where I was. I didn't know why I was here.

Dropping to my knees on the threadbare rug in the little room at the end of the hall, I sent up a prayer.

I prayed for Alexander.

CHAPTER 3

ALEXANDER

I didn't speak as I stumbled from the room and made my way to our private quarters. Clara was in every room I passed through and still gone. Her little touches were all over the parlour: red roses on the side table—a sentimental gesture, a book she was reading on the sofa, photos of us with Elizabeth. The bedroom was worse but I found myself there like a lost dog searching for home. Her perfume lingered in the air, her robe lay across the bed. I'd chastised her once for not allowing the housekeeping staff in here as often as she should, but Clara had wanted privacy, especially in the evenings. As I picked up the silk robe, I found myself thankful she was so stubbornly independent.

She wasn't here. I knew she wouldn't be. But here, in the most private room in the palace, I felt her presence most strongly while feeling her absence even more. The two sensations warred within me, pulling me in two different directions. I pressed her robe to my face, breathing in her scent—roses and vanilla and *home*.

I'd expected it to soothe me—to make me feel closer to her as I tried to process her betrayal. Instead, it brought me to my knees. I crumbled, unable to bear the weight of it, as I buried my face into her scent. Tears broke free as I spilled open clutching the silk as though I might find her there somehow.

But she was gone.

She was lost.

I'd failed. I'd promised to protect her, and I had failed. I'd obsessed and I'd planned and she had still been taken. And in her place there was nothing. Her absence stretched before me like a black hole, sucking me into it slowly. It took my control first. It took my faith next. Then it took my hope and left nothing but a shell concealing the splintered remains of my heart.

That was all I was now without her.

My fingers fumbled on the silk, seeking her out and knowing they'd never touch her again. Soon, her scent would fade from it. Soon she would fade from my life, but never my memories. Soon that was what Clara would become: a collection of moments remembered.

The robe fell from my hands as bile burned up my throat. I retched onto the floor until I was as physically empty as I felt.

The door opened and Edward peered in at me. His eyes found the pile of sick and the robe lying next to it. He didn't speak as he crossed to me and knelt. My arms found my brother and clung to him.

"We're going to find her," he promised me softly.

"What if we don't?" I asked. There were more permutations to this question. What if we did but it was too late? What if he found her and she was…? What if we were wrong? What if we couldn't?

"We will," he said with the conviction of a man who hadn't had his soul stripped from his body. I had no strength left to believe, and I forced myself to draw from his. "Maybe you should lie down."

I shook my head. There would be no rest without her. Part of me wanted to crawl into the bed we shared and lose myself to memories of her body pressed to mine. Part of me wanted to burn this room to the ground. Neither would bring her back to me.

There was no faith left inside me, but searching myself I found something more valuable: determination. Cold, unyielding determination. I didn't know what had happened to my wife, but I knew what I would do to get her back. There were no lengths I wouldn't go to find her. There was no crime I wouldn't commit. There was no sin too great and no sacrifice too large. I would do anything. I was capable of anything. And when I found who took her, I would crush the life from them myself. One person. Ten. A hundred. It would be my hands that stole their last breath.

"Find Smith," I said, "Brex. Georgia. I need to speak to them alone."

"And me?" Edward asked without a hint of frustration. He'd been kept out of plenty of private meetings.

This time it was up to him to decide. "You need to know how far I'll take this. I will do anything to get her back."

"I know," he said quickly. "Me, too."

I drew back and studied him, wondering if that was true and then considering whether I could allow that. "Edward, I know that, but if that's true, maybe it shouldn't be. Can you live with yourself if you killed someone?"

"Can you?" he asked.

"I already do," I said quietly. I'd killed men before—at war and at home. Deaths that had gone untried. Ones that remained unsolved. I didn't go into details. Edward wouldn't be able to stomach them.

As it was, his throat slid as he swallowed my confession. I could see the struggle within him. He loved Clara like she was his own sister. I knew he would do anything to help me save her.

"Clara wouldn't want you to hurt someone for her. She'd never forgive me if I let you."

"And will she forgive you if you hurt someone? If you kill someone?" He tripped over the question and I had my answer. Edward would rise to whatever sin I needed him to commit, but I didn't need him to do that. Not when I was willing. Not when there were plenty of people around us who could live with that decision.

"It doesn't matter," I said curtly. "I don't need my wife's forgiveness, I need her home."

"I don't want to sit around and be useless. I've had enough of that for a lifetime," Edward said bitterly. I wondered how much of his venom was directed at our father and how much I'd earned.

"There's plenty you can do." Things that wouldn't

involved blood on his hands. "Someone needs to look after Sarah and Belle. Someone needs to keep them calm."

"For how long?" he asked, sighing.

I'd expected him to argue with me, but today wasn't a time to take a stand. It was time for us all to fall in line. It was time for us to take our places. "However long it takes."

There wasn't enough room in my study for us to properly plan, and there was the matter of privacy. It was dawn when we assembled in an old conference room once used to brief my grandfather on matters during the war. There were a number of reasons the room was ideal. A large conference table occupied the centre space, allowing us all a seat at the table, and a large bulletin board hung on the wall. It was a relic from the days of maps and strategising moves. I made a mental note to bring in computers.

"A war room?" Brex asked looking around the space. "How far are we going with this?"

"We need the privacy," I said, unfastening my cufflinks so I could roll up my sleeves. Someone, probably Edward, had suggested a shower, but there was no time to waste. No one here had slept. No one here had showered. They were soldiers waiting for the orders of their King and I wasn't going to show even a hint of weakness or privilege. "I don't want this getting out."

"We're not going to be able to contain this information indefinitely," Brex said, turning a chair around so that he could straddle it.

"Then I suggest we find my wife quickly," I snapped. I'd taken my fear and pain and packed it away where it wouldn't cripple me any longer. "Let me be clear, there's only one way this ends: with Clara coming home. I don't care what we have to do. I don't care who we have to get in bed with. There is *nothing* I won't do. Are we clear?"

Each of my three companions nodded.

"If any of you are unwilling to get your hands dirty, you should leave. I won't hold it against you." No one stood. No one walked. I'd expected as much, but it was important to me to know that they were here willingly. Each of them we're capable of murder. Each of them had killed before. But times and people changed. "I know I'm asking too much of you."

"You know why we're here," Georgia muttered.

We were a family—a strange, twisted family but one with tighter bonds than blood could grant, although in a way, it had been blood that bound us—other people's blood. We'd had it on our hands. Some in war. Some in conspiracy. We'd all done it for some perversion of King and Country. Not it was time to soak our hands in crimson once more. This time for our Queen.

"This was a well-organised attack," Smith said, leaning back in his chair. "I hope you trust the people in this room."

"I do." I knew what he was getting at.

"It's unlikely it could be pulled off without multiple people on the inside," he said. "You need to check everyone."

"I already ordered that," Georgia said, earning a sharp

look from Brex. Her eyes narrowed at the unspoken accusation on his face. "You weren't around to do it. Someone had to think."

"Thank you," I said to cut off the argument at its head. "If it's true, then we need to move a few people. Brex, you know who we can trust. Reassign them to my family's personal guard. Elizabeth, Edward, Sarah—I want to know who's watching them."

He nodded. "I know who to move."

"Good. I still—"

"And my wife?" Smith interrupted me. His gaze burned across the room. "I nearly lost her once protecting this family."

"If you don't want to do this," I said coolly.

"I didn't say that. I already threw my lot in," he reminded me, "but my wife is pregnant, too, and I have to place a higher priority on her safety. Actually, it's my highest priority."

Georgia raised an eyebrow, but if she expected me to rebuke him, she was surprised. I expected nothing less of a man like Smith Price. It was why I'd grown to trust him. He was the only man who came close to showing the same consuming love for his wife that I felt for Clara. It meant he was capable of the same dark actions I was, although I didn't fool myself into believing he would go as far as I would to save my wife. Still, he'd gone farther than most already.

Every soul in this room had, and that's why they were here.

"Do you want one of my men? You're welcome to them, but…"

Smith seemed to consider this. He'd been the one to point out that we likely had multiple traitors in our midst. Taking my security would be like playing Russian roulette with his wife. "Georgia?"

"I know someone." That seemed to settle the matter. Given their connections and past, I didn't want to know more about it.

"You want to contain this," Brex said, bringing our conversation around again. "I don't see how. Or for that matter, why."

"Because it will be a shit show," Georgia said flatly. "We won't be able to sneeze without the media catching it on camera."

"But we can't pretend like nothing's happened," he said.

"He's got a point. We can't delay the news of my grandmother's death. So while unfortunate, that will prove a distraction. It will also point interest at Clara." I cleared my throat and relayed what the doctor had said about my grandmother's pills. "It might simply be a heart attack, but the doctor seemed to think it was more."

"How deep does this rabbit hole go?" Brex gave a low whistle, but he looked anything save amused.

"Would Clara do that?" Smith asked and we all turned to stare at him. He held up his hands. "She seems nice, but we haven't spent a lot of quality alone time together."

"I'm glad to hear it," I said. Just the thought of my wife alone with another man scratched at my nerves. I fought against an image of a man touching her now. "No. My wife did not poison my grandmother."

"No one would blame her if she did," Georgia pointed out.

That was true. Mary wasn't well-liked amongst the family. Or the public. Or, well, anyone who'd met her. "It's just poor timing."

"Is it?" Brex asked. He and Smith shared a dark look.

"Out with it," I ordered.

"Your grandmother's heart attack was a pretty big distraction. It shut the whole party down," Smith explained. "You went with her without thinking."

"I have a plan in place," I snapped, slightly insulted that he thought so little of me. "I sent Norris with her. He followed protocol and maintained contact until he went radio silent."

"That's the problem. You followed protocol. In case of emergency, the Queen is evacuated, correct?"

"Of course."

"Like the day of the Child Watch attack?" He'd found the piece of the puzzle that fit and it made the haphazard ones suddenly fall into place.

"We didn't know why the symposium was attacked," Brex said. "No one was hurt. What was the point?"

"It wasn't an attack." The room spun for a moment as I realized what we'd been missing.

"It was a dress rehearsal." Georgia slammed a fist onto the table, but none of us jumped. We didn't have any surprise left in us.

We'd considered every angle regarding the explosion at

the Child Watch symposium my wife had attended in January, but now it seemed obvious. Whoever was behind it—behind this—hadn't been looking to hurt anyone. My wife had been a target, but not in the way I'd thought.

"But we didn't follow protocol," Brex pointed out.

"Because Clara was being stubborn, and then you showed up." Georgia pointed a finger at me.

I had arrived that day only moments after the first bomb had detonated. I'd come as soon as I heard there was possible danger—and someone had noticed.

"Fuck," I roared. I'd handed them all the information they needed: who I trusted, who surrounded me and my family, and how I would react if my wife was in danger.

"They needed to keep you occupied," Smith said.

"So they poisoned my grandmother." It made sense in a twisted way. I'd gone with her automatically, trained to respond to my family's needs in the way I'd been bred for.

"But what about Clara and the medication? I don't see how that fits," Brex admitted.

"They're thumbing their noses at us." Georgia laughed humourlessly. "There will be an inquisition into Mary's death. The doctor knows that Clara handled the pills. Basically, they're sending a giant fuck you. They know we can't hide that Clara's gone and what are people going to think?"

"She didn't have anything to do with my grandmother's death." Anger rose hot inside me and squeezed my heart. It was ridiculous to even consider the possibility.

"But how will it look when she doesn't respond or agree to questioning?"

"They want us to admit that she's gone."

"But without proof, people will think..." Brex trailed away as though deciding it wasn't worth it to point out the obvious.

"That she's guilty." It was a brilliant maneuver that had been played so subtly. I hadn't seen it for what it was. Now, though, all the mechanisms were clear. Someone had set up these events like a string of dominoes. How many had yet to fall?

"Maybe we can spin it to our advantage," Smith said.

"How?" Georgia asked. It was a damn good question.

"Let the scandal unfold. Claim the Queen is horrified. Leak stories to the media about how she won't leave the house," he suggested.

"The public will crucify her," Brex said.

"But their focus will stay on that." I was beginning to see where he was going with this. I didn't like it, especially given what it meant for my role in this.

"You're going to have to distract them, Poor Boy, and let us go to work," Brex said, sounding apologetic.

"That's why we're here." I gestured to the same around us. "You three can move about freely, but my own movements will be watched."

"Aren't the King's moves always analysed?" Georgia said dryly.

"Thankfully, this isn't a chess match. We've been at war before and the Royal family was prepared." Moving to the bulletin board I pressed a spot where an invisible button offered a solution to my problem. In the corner, the tile floor dropped an inch and slid open to reveal a staircase that led down.

"Where does that go?" Brex shot me a look that clearly indicated that he didn't approve of not knowing about this.

"Only the monarch knows about this," I explained, "until now. The King has a bit more freedom of movement than anyone outside this room knows."

"I hope we're all trustworthy," Smith said. He seemed the least impressed by this revelation.

"I don't doubt a single person in this room's loyalty." It was less important to say that than it was to imply what I hadn't said.

"And the rest of them?" Georgia asked, slowly catching on to my meaning.

"I want them watched, particularly my uncle." He'd been the one to ask Clara to handle that medication. His reappearance in my life had come on the heels of the Child Watch attack. In all honesty, it felt too easy. But if Henry wasn't responsible, someone near him had to be involved. "Keep him in London."

Georgia nodded that she understood the order.

"Alexander, what about Norris?" Brex asked.

I'd carefully left him out of most of our conversations, because as difficult as it was to face Clara's disappearance, I'd primed myself to expect something to happen to her. I'd never considered that anything could befall Norris.

"Could he turn?" Smith asked. His question was met with three glares. "I guess not."

"He would never," Georgia said, anger coloring her voice.

Smith shrugged his broad shoulders. "I hope you're right about that."

"We are," Brex assured him.

"I'm glad to hear it." Smith sounded sincere, but he hesitated for a moment. "It's just that if he's not involved, where is he?"

If my heart was still in my chest, it might have hurt more to face what I knew to be true. There was only one explanation for why Norris had gone silent. But there was simply a gaping hole where it had been ripped from me and no pain left to feel. "Dead."

"He might not..." Georgia began softly before losing conviction.

None of us wanted to believe Norris was gone. I still expected him to come striding into the room full of criticism for how I was handling the situation. But enough time had passed that I no longer believed he would. Later, I would grieve for him. Later, I would face the terrible loss. At the moment, my place was here, as his would have been. "Norris would want us to find Clara. That's what he would be doing now."

Georgia nodded in agreement, looking utterly stricken by the thought of his death.

"I won't believe it until I bury his body." Brex was as stubborn as I was, maybe more-so. I wished I could hold out some hope, but all of it had been taken from me. "Why would they kill him and not kill—"

"Because they wouldn't," Georgia cut him off before he could voice the fear that remained unspoken.

The air around us thickened as the words remained unsaid, until Smith finally offered a bit of logic. "Why would they kill her? It doesn't make sense. There's no leverage if she's dead. Capturing her makes more sense."

I wanted to be comforted by this, but the thought of my wife and death in the same sentence made that impossible.

"We won't be able to do this alone," Smith said, shifting directions. "Is it possible the Council of Ghosts is involved?"

Brex looked at him like he was speaking gibberish. "Council of what now?"

"Smith and I recently met a legend—the Council of Ghosts," I explained. "Unofficially known as the Kingmakers."

"You mean?" He scratched the back of his neck.

"Sometimes monarchs need to be deposed and they tend to be the ones to decide that," Smith said matter-of-factly. It must be easier for him to consider their role in the assassinations of the rulers before me. I found it more unsettling.

"Did you piss them off?" Georgia asked.

"No." I shook my head. "But they might be able to help. They're powerful and they have a number of ties to people who know things."

"I didn't get the impression that they were interested in being your new best friends," Smith pointed out.

That was true, but I had to consider every weapon in my arsenal, and the Council of Ghosts wasn't even the most dangerous one.

"I'll set up a meeting," I said. "In the meantime, Brex?"

"I'll review the security footage with Georgia and pull up the CCTV around the museum. There are eyes everywhere in London. We just have to find the right ones." His confidence bolstered mine, but I knew it was false bravado. He stood and waited for Georgia.

She paused for a moment, opening and closing her mouth like she was going to say something but kept losing her nerve. It was very un-Georgia-like. "Yes?"

"I just found out about the baby," she said. "Clara was going to tell you. I thought you should know that. I don't think she wanted to accept it herself."

"I'm not angry with my wife," I said smoothly. I didn't have any anger left for Clara. Not right now. Georgia looked at me like she wanted to say more, but instead she followed Brex away from our new, unofficial strategy room.

"Should we see the Ghosts?" I asked Smith. I hated how unclear the path before me was, and I could only hope he was thinking more clearly than me. I had more means at my disposal than most men alive—that didn't mean I could always call on them.

"We could," he hedged. If he resented losing an entire night's sleep, he didn't show it. Then again, he'd kept odd hours when he'd played attorney to the city's criminal elite. He was used to this and used to dealing with them. That's why I kept him with me now. "There's someone else we should see first."

"Who?"

"You aren't going to like it," he warned me.

"Where are we going?" I stood, already determined to make the call. I knew once I did that I couldn't take it back. But when I'd said I would do anything to get Clara back, I'd meant it.

I thought back to the day we'd met the Council of Ghosts. He'd asked me how far as I was willing to go to end this. I'd thought then that I knew my absolute limit.

It seemed Smith planned to test that. "I asked you if you would sell your soul once. It's time to meet the devil."

CHAPTER 4
CLARA

I gave up. After the girl ran, I'd gone up and down the dark corridor, checking doors, but none of them opened. Whoever she was—if she were even real—she was gone. There was no sign of anyone else, either, but I couldn't be alone. If someone wanted me dead, I would be. I'd been helpless when they knocked me out and brought me here. But I'd woken up, which meant someone wanted me alive. It wasn't a very comforting thought but it was all I had. Eventually someone would come to me and explain why I was here. They would bring me food. I could reason with them.

I could beg.

I told myself these things to stay calm, because I knew that if I let myself think about this too long...

So, I waited, door open, in the little room where I'd found the clothes, where I'd seen the girl. Part of me wanted to shut the door and push the chest of drawers against it. I wanted to hunker down until Alexander found me.

I imagined him here now, his arms wrapping around me. I could almost feel his strong body pressed to mine—see that self-assured smirk flash across his face. My fingers brushed over my stomach, wishing they were in his hair as he swept me into a relieved kiss. I closed my eyes and for a moment I could swear I caught his scent—bergamot and vetiver and something indescribably him. I knew when I opened my eyes the false peace I'd felt would evaporate. He wasn't here. I wasn't safe.

I didn't want to face it, but I couldn't ignore what I'd seen when I'd paced the hall—or, rather, what I hadn't. There were no windows. No signs of light. The doors in the corridor were heavy and reinforced. One of them must have led out and I didn't want to know what lay behind the others. I hadn't learned much by exploring except one thing: I was a prisoner. And wherever I'd been taken was secure.

So how was he going to find me?

I swallowed against a swell of panic. Freaking out wasn't going to help, and there was the baby to consider. I'd been drugged and forced here that was more than enough stress. I couldn't add anymore to the baby's heart.

I was about to wander down the hall again and hope to spot a clue when a smiling woman appeared in the door.

She tugged at her white nurse's uniform and my adrenaline spiked. Why would she wear that? My hands covered my swollen belly protectively.

I should have barricaded the door. I should have waited for Alexander to come.

"Would you come with me, Ms. Bishop?" She asked in a pleasant voice as though I'd just been called in from the waiting room at the doctor's office. But this was wrong. This was all wrong.

"I'm married," I said coldly.

"Our files indicate that you aren't. My apologies."

Was she kidding? I stared at her, waiting for her to crack and show that she knew who I was. Because how couldn't she? But she didn't look away. She didn't smirk or frown. She simply returned my stare with a blank expression. "Where do you think this came from?"

"I'm not one to judge." She stepped to the side and smiled wider. The shadows of the corridor washed away everything but the whites of her eyes and her teeth.

I held my stomach tighter. "I'm not going anywhere until you tell me where I am."

"The doctor insists on checking on the baby. You had a traumatic event and with the baby's heart condition, a test would be prudent."

My own heart shuttered to a stop. Whatever their warped files said, *that* was correct. They knew about the baby, so why lie about who I was? I couldn't trust her. I couldn't trust this doctor. But I was out of options. I'd tried the other doors. I'd combed every inch of space available to me. What other choice did I have if I wanted to see where one of those other doors led?

"And if I don't cooperate?" I asked, already expecting her answer.

"I'll have to sedate you." The smile slipped replaced by a disapproving scowl. "The doctor is quite insistent these tests be performed."

Sedation meant I wouldn't see where they took me or who performed the tests. It meant losing out on valuable information. It meant I had to play along, even if I wanted to fight. But it also meant I'd be awake and if this doctor or anyone else tried to hurt me or the baby, they wouldn't know what hit them. No one was going to hurt me or my child.

"Fine," I agreed.

She moved into the doorway, her unsettling grin returning, and waited for me. The corridor looked the same. There was no open door. No sign of where she'd come from. I followed her a few paces before she paused at a door. *Across the hall from my room and two down.* I made a mental note. The nurse paused a second before a loud whir and click echoed through the empty space. It had been unlocked automatically by someone else. Someone who was watching us —that was going to make things more difficult.

"Why am I here?" I asked her again, hesitating at the threshold. Fear tugged at me from both sides. Whatever was on the other side of this door could be my salvation or my destruction. But staying put wasn't an option. It was nothing more than the illusion of safety. No matter that I found on the other side, I could turn it to my advantage. I had to.

She patted my arm sympathetically, shaking her head. "That's above my clearance."

Clearance? That was an odd choice of words. I tucked the thought away. I needed to stay alert. I needed to figure out where I was and how to escape. Maybe that started with finding an ally.

"What's your name?" I switched tactics. Norris told me once that people loved to talk about themselves. He'd said that friendly conversation spilled more secrets than interrogation. I hoped he was right—I hoped he was okay.

"June." She hustled me through the door, still acting like this was a normal day at the office. But this wasn't normal. None of it was, so how could she act like this?

As I walked through the unlocked door, things got stranger.

CHAPTER 5
ALEXANDER

I didn't ask where we were going. I suspected I didn't want to know. I'd meant it when I said I would do anything and partner with anyone to see Clara safely home. My body felt hollow as though some vital life force had been torn from me. In its place a flame flickered to life. I didn't know where the spark had come from but it fueled me now. It drove me forward when most of me wanted to crumble from the loss. Perhaps, it was denial. Maybe it was love. I didn't care as long as nothing extinguished it.

"Let's take mine. The press will follow your cars," Smith advised as we neared the private car park where a half dozen Range Rovers and a few other employee vehicles waited.

"You're probably right," I agreed. They would be camped out and more vicious than usual after news of my grandmother's death leaked. "The last thing I need is an over-eager paparazzi to catch a photo of me meeting with a criminal."

"How do you know I'm taking you to see a criminal?" Smith asked pulling keys from his pocket.

"I assume the devil isn't a saint," I said flatly.

I didn't have to ask him which one was his. Another day I might have been impressed by the black Bugatti. Today, the ostentatious display of wealth didn't register.

I was fire and ice—burning and numb at once.

"This won't get noticed?" I asked, suddenly uncertain of his plan's wisdom.

"It will get noticed," Smith said with a hollow laugh. "But people will be staring at the car. Not you."

It helped that the windows were tinted far beyond any legal limit. The engine roared to life as I slid into my seat. We left out a back gate, Smith pulling into the morning traffic smoothly. I averted my eyes, but I felt them there: the reporters, the gawkers, the tourists. They all wanted a glimpse of me—of my life.

A gate. A fence. Castle walls. They weren't enough. I hated the lack of boundaries. I hated that every move I made had to be choreographed to avoid speculation. I hated that I'd assumed the throne to protect my family.

I hated the glass crown I wore—invisible but heavy, powerful but impotent. It meant nothing. None of this did. I'd chosen a life of duty and fate had rewarded me with pain.

Smith didn't attempt conversation. We'd bandied theories and strategies with the others for hours. I needed time to be with my own thoughts. I suspected he did, too. But as we drove further, leaving the city behind, I was no closer to understanding what had happened.

When we reached Surrey, I expected to find myself at a quaint old estate. Instead, Smith turned down a long drive. The tree-lined path was broken only by a small guard station. There was no house in sight.

Smith stopped the car and rolled down the window. "Smith Price."

"Is he expecting you?" The guard asked.

"I believe I'm on the list," Smith said dryly.

A moment later, we were on our way. The trees grew denser for a moment, shielding the home that lay beyond and when we finally passed them, I found myself staring at a home that rivaled the grandeur of most crown estates. Unlike my family's holdings, this was clearly a newly built residence. The circular drive was paved with smooth stone and a fountain gurgled in its centre. The villa beyond belonged in Italy not outside London with its terra-cotta shingled roof and sprawling mass.

I didn't have to ask him where we were. I'd seen this house before in briefings with MI-5. It was burned into my brain.

"So this is hell." I said absently.

"Were you expecting more flames?" Smith asked. He pulled to the entrance and parked the Bugatti with a familiarity.

He'd been here before. Of course, he had. He'd worked for Hammond and a number of other unsavoury London businessmen.

"Strangely, no." If there was a hell on earth—or, at least, England—it was the DeAngelo family estate.

The DeAngelos were one of London's primary crime

syndicates. I'd been briefed on their activities on a number of occasions. They murdered, plotted, laundered money— and I'd just driven into the belly of the beast.

Two massive wooden doors loomed ahead. Once I walked through them, there would be no turning back.

"Do we knock?" I asked Smith as we reached the doors.

As in answer, one creaked open and a security guard motioned us inside. He was dressed in a black suit that did nothing to hide his paunch or the gun holstered under his left arm.

"Please." He motioned for me to spread my arms and legs.

My eyebrows shot up. I couldn't remember the last time I was frisked. In fact, I might never have been frisked. "I don't carry a weapon."

That fact didn't matter to him. If he knew who he was, and the chances were minuscule that he didn't, he acted oblivious as he swept his hands under my arms and up my legs.

When he turned to my companion, Smith handed the man a small pistol. "Here."

This must have engendered trust because Smith escaped the pat-down. It didn't surprise me that he carried a gun.

"This way." The guard tipped his head and we followed through a marble lined corridor.

"You should carry a weapon," Smith advised.

"I left the guns in Afghanistan," I muttered. The thought had occurred to me, too, but I'd clung to the idea that something in my life could be normal. I couldn't have been more wrong and my blind arrogance had cost me.

"Whatever this game is," Smith continued in a low voice, aware that the guard was probably listening to every word we said, "the stakes have gone up. You should be prepared, especially now that..."

He didn't finish the statement, but I knew what he was driving at. With Norris missing, I was vulnerable in a way I'd never been before. He'd carried a gun. Everyone on my team did.

I'd pretended for a long time that my place in the grand scheme was different. I was a father, a husband, a king. I'd let myself hover in the shadows on the board while I moved the other players, gambling their lives in exchange for my protection.

For the Queen's protection.

And someone had outplayed me.

They might again. I couldn't be caught unprepared next time. "I'll have Brex get one."

"That would be wise."

The man showed us into a large sitting room where two men in suits occupied seats parallel to one another. Outside the picture windows, a rolling green lawn stretched to the edge of a forest. It was the picture of civility—and it was a lie. Nothing about the DeAngelo family or their associates was civil.

"Are we interrupting?" Smith asked.

"No." The older man brushed off his concern as they both stood. "Mr. Ford and I are finished with our business."

The two shook hands, exchanging farewells with such ease, I might have thought they'd simply had afternoon tea.

"Your Majesty." The younger man, Ford, nodded as he passed but didn't seem ruffled to discover that the King of England was meeting with a mob boss. He also didn't display a hint of humility. Instead, he prowled past us, exiting the room and returning to whatever dark world he inhabited.

"Smith Price. I didn't expect to see you walk through my doors." Marcus DeAngelo's eyes skimmed over me, tightening at the edges before they skipped to my companion. It was the only sign of surprise at my presence. "I'd hoped you came to accept my job offer, but it looks as if you've found another organisation in which to invest your talents."

"I'm retired," Smith said.

"So I've heard." DeAngelo paused to pour himself a drink. Each moment of delay irked me. We were wasting time while playing at niceties with a known criminal. "But here you are—and with such auspicious company. It seems you've found a new family."

"I suppose I went legit."

"I wouldn't say that," DeAngelo said. He lifted the crystal decanter in offering.

I wanted a drink, which was why I shouldn't have one. I needed to keep my mind sharp, especially in the presence of a wolf.

"No, thank you." I shifted on my heels. It was difficult to be polite to a man who actively worked against my country, who ran weapons and controlled drug trafficking. It was hard to ignore that those were the least of his sins.

DeAngelo waved to a set of leather cigar chairs. "Sit, gentleman."

He wasn't the type to use my title. I wasn't the type to take an order.

"He asked nicely," Smith said under his breath, sensing my dilemma.

And I was the one who'd agreed to come.

"What trouble brings you to my door?" DeAngelo swished his bourbon thoughtfully while he waited for us to respond.

"Why do you assume there's trouble?" Smith asked nonchalantly. He might not practice anymore, but he was still a lawyer.

"If you came to me for help, I assume there must be trouble. Particularly, given..." DeAngelo leveled a long look at me.

It was an odd game we were playing, skirting around the fact that he and I were connected by more than this spontaneous meeting. DeAngelo didn't seem interested in keeping that information close to the vest.

Smith had obviously been expecting a different reaction. He looked between us, his eyebrows drawing together. "What?"

"He must be new to your circle," DeAngelo drawled, "if he doesn't know."

"It's not common knowledge that you provided the gun that killed my father," I said coolly. If he was going to show his hand, I might as well. The king beat most cards, after all.

"That complicates things," Smith said, shooting me a look.

It wasn't my fault that I hadn't told him. I didn't know where we were going. But I was lying to myself if I pretended that I hadn't suspected where he was bringing us.

Smith had been part of the investigation that had led from Jack Hammond to Oliver Jacobson. He knew more than most about my father's assassination, but I'd never shared the information about the gun. It hadn't seemed important. Then again, I didn't know he associated with the DeAngelo family.

"Does it?" DeAngelo said, his lips twitching. "It was a business transaction. Much like the one I expect we'll conduct this afternoon."

"MI-5 would rather nail him for something larger," I explained to Smith, my eyes remaining on DeAngelo. Smith was wrong. This man wasn't the devil, but he'd sold his soul to him—and hell would come to collect eventually. No man could play with fire forever without getting burned.

"Yes, they would." He didn't seem the least bit ruffled by this fact. Maybe he always knew he was on borrowed time. Maybe that's why he did it.

"There's been a security breach," Smith said, "and we're wondering what you know about some recent events."

"The bombing of that symposium, I assume?"

Ice trickled down my neck. It couldn't be coincidence that he would bring that up. Not now that we knew that there was so much more to that day than a failed attack. It took effort to keep my voice measured. Almost as much effort as it did to stop myself from grabbing him and pounding the information out of him. "Yes. We believe there might be a group plotting against the crown."

"When isn't there?" he snorted.

I slammed my fist on the side table, barely aware of the jolt it sent bursting through my nerves. "This isn't a joke."

Silence fell over us for a moment as we regarded each other. On one side, I sat: the very symbol of this nation's law and order. Across from me, DeAngelo stared back at me like a mirror: the opposite of me—chaotic and self-serv-ing. And between: a man who belonged to neither of us, who acted in his own interest according to a moral compass I didn't always understand. We were a spectrum of morality that twisted back on itself like a Mobius strip. I was as capable of selfish action as DeAngelo. I would do anything and hurt anyone to get Clara back. I could only hope the same was true for him—that he was capable of benevolence.

"Who did they hurt?" Marcus asked shrewdly. He still hadn't taken a drink. It was a clutch, a prop to hide some nervous tick or behaviour. Like me, he has no interesting in dulling his faculties in mixed company.

"An advisor," I said quickly, exchanging looks with Smith. He hadn't clarified why he was involving London's reigning mob boss, but telling him that Clara was missing had the potential for disastrous consequences.

DeAngelo abandoned his drink on the table and leaned forward to rest his palms on his knees. "Lying to me will only get you half the information you need."

"You don't need to know more than that," Smith said firmly, stepping into the role of my counsel once more.

"Fine." The older man settled back, looking nonplussed by this refusal. "Be that as it may, it won't help me determine who finally acted."

His words landed on my chest and I felt a hollow pang. There were always groups plotting against the government. This was something more. This was personal. I felt it deep in my bones. This wasn't terrorism of anyone but me. A series of events had been set in motion that served to punish my family, but I couldn't understand why.

"You've shaken things up a bit since taking the throne. Now, I wholly approve," DeAngelo added.

"Is my approval rating affected by the lack of charges brought against you?" I asked flatly. I'd questioned once what my father would have done with the information we had about his involvement. It was telling that the murder of a king rated lower than the other crimes he'd committed. I didn't know if that said more about where the royal family stood or more about his sins.

"Others aren't quite as thrilled," DeAngelo continued, "I wouldn't be surprised to find out the Council of Ghosts was involved."

"They aren't," I said curtly. There was no reason for them to act—not in this fashion. If the Kingmakers, the secret council of MPs that deposed monarchs according to their whims, wanted to take action, it would have been against me. Not Clara.

"If you're that sure, you must have met them." When I didn't respond, he shrugged. "There are other groups—domestic terrorists, foreign terrorists. I still can't help but wonder why you've come to me."

He knew something. It was why he kept returning to that fact. He knew what we didn't, and he wouldn't be happy until we admitted.

"Did you have something to do with it?" Smith asked bluntly.

DeAngelo barked a laugh, shaking his head, as though he'd just heard a good joke. "You're going to hurt my feelings. I harbour no ill will against the Crown. Why would a powerful man concern himself with an impotent dog?"

That's what he thought of me. Of us. Our inaction was a sign of weakness. "The monarchy has been more than willing to overlook your involvement in the King's assassination. Perhaps that decision should be reversed."

"Will MI-5 allow it?" he asked coldly.

"They'll do as I instruct," I countered.

"Are you sure? Don't you do as they instruct? The king might be an impotent cur, but he's well-trained."

I was on my feet before the last insult left his mouth. "You'll find I'm not like my father. I don't send other men to do my dirty work."

"And that's why you're here." DeAngelo shrank a little in his chair. "Sit down before my guards come in and misinterpret the situation."

"I've been shot before," I reminded him in a low voice.

"I'm betting I could crush your windpipe before they hit me more than twice."

DeAngelo blinked, then a catlike smile carved across his face. "You aren't like your father. That's good. You're going to need some piss and vinegar in you if you plan to keep upending the country. Now sit down and let's discuss this trouble. I don't deal with men who aren't willing to fight their own battles.

He'd been testing me, and I'd passed. A quick glance at Smith confirmed that he'd known this all along. I wondered if either of them knew how close I'd come to acting on my threat.

"You'll help us," Smith said as though nothing had happened.

"For a price. Everything comes with a price," he said, "especially information."

My mind immediately went to money. I had money. It turned my stomach to consider paying the man that had been integral in my father's death—the man whose actions had brought me here.

But Smith was a lawyer, who specialised in dealing with men like DeAngelo. "Would you consider a barter?"

"If there's information of value."

"I could insist the same," Smith countered.

"I suppose one of us has to gamble," DeAngelo said. "I might be able to help you. You might be able to help me. But only one of us came looking for help."

"The name of the man working with MI-5," Smith offered, "if you have something of value."

He'd just signed someone's death certificate without

blinking. I knew the name. Smith must have guessed based on our early conversation. It wasn't a difficult leap to make, but it was a bluff all the same. How else could I have known about the gun or that MI-5 was actively investigating DeAngelo?

DeAngelo's shoulders locked, his eyes darkening to black beads. Finally, we had his interest. "I can give you a theory and point you in a direction. You'll want to talk to MI-18 for the rest."

"There is no MI-18," I said quickly.

"It's an insult to both of us to lie," DeAngelo said.

"That's not enough to buy a name." Smith didn't concern himself with debating the existence or nonexistence of a military intelligence department.

DeAngelo clucked, dropping his rigid shoulders. He knew he had us, which meant it was only a matter of time before we turned over what he wanted. "I haven't laid out my theory. What do you know about the Colony?"

"That was pointless," I muttered, throwing open the Bugatti's door and earning a sharp look from Smith. I suspected he would betray me in a heart beat if this bloody car was in jeopardy.

So why did I trust him? Why was I relying on a man who valued life so little?

"Was it?" Smith slid behind the wheel. "I didn't think so."

"I gathered that when you sold out Ethan Small." I felt dirty for giving the name. I'd prepared myself to go as far as

I had to in order to find Clara, but it felt different to have acted.

"A price had to be paid." Smith left the words hanging, a reminder that I'd had a choice and I'd chosen to sign the cheque. "You can't question the choices you made after the fact," he advised, pulling around the circular drive and waiting for the gates to open.

I'd known. I'd do it again. "I'm not."

"Ethan Small hand-delivered the gun that killed your father," Smith reminded me.

"And he felt so guilty about it that he's been cooperating with us ever since."

"Wanting to avoid jail time is not cooperating. His life for Clara's isn't even a question." Something in his voice dared me to disagree. I was being tested again.

"Let me be clear. No one will stand between me reaching her. *No one.*" There wasn't a single person in this world that I wouldn't trade for my wife and children's safety. "Including you or your wife or our friends."

"Fair enough." This revelation rolled off Smith's shoulders. Possibly, because he would betray any of us for Belle.

It was why we trusted each other. It was why we worked together. It was also why we'd never be friends.

Knowing that made it easier to shift attention back to our current situation."If this Colony is real, there's one place to start asking questions."

"I assume you mean Oliver Jacobson," Smith spat out the name. "What about our other lead? Or are you going to try to sell me that MI-18 doesn't exist, too?"

"You knew?" I asked, not trying to hide my disbelief.

There were few more well-guarded secrets than its existence. Technically, even I wasn't supposed to know.

"No," Smith admitted, turning the Bugatti in the direction of London, "but there was no reason for DeAngelo to bluff on that point."

I hadn't given DeAngelo an inch on MI-18. Everyone knew about MI-5 and MI-6. There were a number of other sections, some in operation, most defunct. As far as the other departments, the public, even the monarchy were concerned, military intelligence section 18 had never been utilised. But MI-18 had been in continuous operation since the second world war when it had become necessary to track individuals and groups with more revolutionary tastes. The people undermining the allies while hiding in British fallout shelters.

"Strictly speaking, I'm not supposed to know about them," I confessed. "It's black ops. Completely covert. No records. No oversight. Only MI-18 knows about MI-18."

"So how do you know?" Smith asked slowly.

I drew a deep breath before answering. I was about to betray a confidence—and it was a secret that could get someone killed. "Norris."

CHAPTER 6

An obnoxious beeping filtered into the darkness. It ricocheted around his brain like a bullet. Blinking his eyes, Norris stared up at a white-tiled ceiling. The word hospital processed in his sluggish mind, but when he went to move, he couldn't. Straining to see, he discovered two thick leather belts buckled around his wrists. He couldn't feel his legs to know if they were similarly bound or worse. Instinct took over and he pulled against the straps as his last few memories filtered back to him.

He'd been at a party. Something had happened.

Mary, Alexander's grandmother had collapsed. He was asked to take the Queen home.

The rest of the night came in scattered pieces.

Clara worried but holding herself together.

Sarah sitting mute and shocked in the backseat.

Moonlight catching the hood of the Range Rover and reflecting something odd.

Then searing pain near his left kidney and Clara's stricken face giving way to blackness.

"Blue."

Clara.

Norris could only hope that he'd managed to catch her attention. He hoped she'd understood what he was trying to say. The Range Rover wasn't theirs. The royal family used exclusively black models. The car that had arrived was blue. Was it enough of a warning? Maybe she'd had time to scream or run. He was in a hospital. Whoever had tried to silence him—or more likely, kill him—failed.

None of that explained why he was tied to the bed.

In Norris's experience, which was considerable, it was never a good thing to wake up in a strange hospital room strapped down.

It took longer than it should have for him to process what that meant. No doubt he'd been under sedation. If he was here, he'd failed. Clara hadn't gotten help. There was no other accounting for the bindings. But what had happened to her?

Taking a moment, he relaxed as best he could and tried not to think about why he couldn't feel his legs. He needed to get his hands free first and foremost. Then, he would worry about his feet. Getting out of leather restraints was tricky, but not impossible. It was a skill he'd picked up before he came to work for Alexander's family. But it had been years since Norris was a special operative and even longer since he'd found himself in this position.

And he didn't have time to waste. He'd have to do it the hard way. The trick was to break the bones fast enough that he could unbuckle the second restraint before swelling made it too difficult.

Breaking bones wasn't exactly a walk in the park either. Twisting his wrist hard, he jammed it against the leather as hard as he could. It was faster with metal handcuffs.

He needed more leverage, but when he tried to move his torso, white-hot lighting shot through his side. A cold sweat broke over his brow and he fell back panting. It was a stab wound, judging by his memory and the way it hurt now, and it wasn't going to make life any easier. This was no time to feel sorry for himself, though. Not while his family was in danger. Resuming his efforts, he was finally rewarded with a splintering crack.

Only a few more and he'd be able to slip his hand free. Next to him a monitor spiked and he cursed. He hadn't been considering his heart rate. Willing it down, he watched it fall a few beats per minute while he continued his manipulations of the cuff.

But it was too late.

A woman in a white lab coat rushed into the room. "Mr. Norris, please control yourself. You're injured."

Norris stilled and considered his position. She didn't know that he'd nearly freed one hand, but the longer she talked, the more swelling would occur and he'd be in worse shape if he had a broken, swollen hand ballooning against the leather.

Still, he needed to gather info. "Undo these and I won't need to struggle. Doctor?"

She didn't correct him. Instead, she made her way to the monitors, her eyes beady as she took in the numbers.

She was younger than him, but not by much. There was no hospital insignia on her lab coat and under it she wore street clothes.

A private physician of some sort. The fact that she didn't give her name was also telling.

"I'm afraid that isn't possible given the circumstances. You've been deemed a flight risk," she informed him, remaining interested in the machines and refusing to speak directly to him.

Norris wasn't entirely certain what to make of her, but his gut feeling wasn't good. Nothing added up here, particularly her.

But why keep him alive? Unless...

"I want to speak to the king. He would never allow this." It was a test.

"Who do you think ordered you here?" She failed it entirely. There was no circumstance under which Alexander would have sent him to be confined to a hospital. But she wasn't through digging her grave. "You're being held on suspicion of conspiracy."

"Conspiracy of what?" He asked quietly. He was running out of time. His hand was beginning to pound.

"Kidnapping, to start," she said. "Attempted murder."

Soon, there would be a real reason to hold him for murder. When he managed to get free, no one would stand in his way.

"I'll send someone in to attend to your hand." She trailed an icy finger along the spot where he'd broken the bone. Norris bit back a yelp. "We're not stupid, Mr. Norris. We're aware of your particular skills."

He didn't bother to comment. If he was stuck here, he might as well get as much information from her as possible. "And the Queen? Is she safe?"

That was all that really matted. If he was being held on conspiracy charges that would be sorted out soon enough. No matter what danger he was in, his family was his primary concern.

She leveled a long look at him. "Why don't you tell us?"

CHAPTER 7

CLARA

The bright lights and white walls felt familiar and safe —I knew I was anything but. On the other side of the unlocked door, I found myself in a standard hospital wing. I felt like Alice falling through the rabbit hole. Nothing was what it seemed here. Not that I had any idea where *here* was. But regardless of the lights and busy clinic, I knew I wasn't safe. There were no windows and every door locked behind me.

There were more people here, though no one looked my way as I passed in my too-small clothes. No one seemed at all interested in my presence. I was a ghost gliding among the living—unseen, unnoticed, uninteresting. I tried to take in small details—the man in the lab coat testing a vial of blood, a series of numbered rooms with tinted glass doors, an empty bed being wheeled by—but there was nothing remarkable about any of it. Its mundanity made it all the more chilling. This could be any clinic if not for the fact that it connected to an anonymous prison and that I hadn't walked in here of my own volition. Then there were the people—presumably, doctors and nurses—did they know I'd been taken? Was everyone here in on my disappearance?

And why? It always came back to that one question: why?

"The doctor will be with you in a moment," June told me as she waved a badge over a card reader and showed me into a room.

Before she had waited until someone unlocked a door. Here, that badge was like waving a magic wand.

She pointed to the exam table and a folded cloth resting on it. I picked it up—it was such an ordinary, familiar thing: a cotton hospital gown. It didn't match with my circumstances. The last time I'd changed into one of these I'd been waiting for my doctor with my best friend by my side.

I fingered the worn fabric, stomach churning as I realized it had been washed many times. What was this place? Maybe none of this was real. Maybe I was trapped in a nightmare.

"Please change into that. I'll see that some clothes are delivered to you. Obviously, someone forgot to see that your quarters were stocked properly." She drew a curtain down the center of the room and waited on the other side.

Her attitude only made things worse. Cheerful, kind—it was as though none of this was wrong. They'd kidnapped me, held me captive, and now I was being treated like...like...

I didn't understand it. I didn't know what I was—something between a guest and a prisoner. I wasn't free to go but

I wasn't being treated poorly. The rumble of my stomach reminded me I wasn't being treated well, either.

"Can I get something to eat?" I asked, rubbing my belly.

"Oh, you poor duck, of course. *After the tests*. It's necessary for you to be in a fasting state," she explained, taking the ill-fitting garments from me. She handed me a cup and pointed to a bathroom.

I knew exactly what to do. I'd done it dozens of times before, but I couldn't continue to pretend this was normal. I wanted answers. I wanted reassurances. I wanted my husband.

"What are they going to do?" I asked, panic finally winning out. "What are they going to do to my baby?"

"Don't you worry about that. You're in good hands," she said calmly. "Everyone deserves the best care no matter what they've done."

Her words stole my breath for a moment. "Done?" I repeated. "What does that mean?"

"I don't have access to more than your medical file, Miss Bishop," she said, "but a woman gets sent here for a reason."

"Where is here?" I felt like a scratched record, repeating the same line over and over, jolting with each skip. "Do you know who I am?"

"Clara Bishop," June said, blinking. She cocked her head and studied me for a moment as though diagnosing me.

"Yes," I said slowly. "I was Clara Bishop. Now I'm the Queen."

"The queen?" Her eyebrows shot up before she began to laugh. "I haven't heard that one before."

Why was she acting like this? Why was she pretending I wasn't who I said I was? She had to know. I hadn't wound up here accidentally. The world began to spin around me—or was I the crazy one? What if I was right? What if none of this was real? What if nothing I believed was true? I stumbled a step, my hand closing over my stomach. The baby kicked and instantly I felt anchored. There was my proof. Alexander's child grew inside me. We'd made this baby with our love—love that was the a living, breathing passion. I felt it now. Even separated, I was always with him. It was his heart in my chest. It was his strength that kept me from falling.

Someone wanted to play a game. I suspected it wasn't June. She wasn't lying. She believed every word she said. But if she knew the truth—if she could be convinced—would she help me?

"It's true. Someone took me," I told her in a rush, clutching her arm. "You have to help me. You can't let them hurt me or my baby."

"No one is going to hurt your baby," she reassured me, dismissing me like I was a hysterical woman. "The doctor will be with you in a moment."

A little bit of my hope died. If she wouldn't help me—if all these people would stand by and treat me like I was a raving lunatic—what could I do?

She pried my fingers free, backing up a few steps and I saw it. *Fear.* Not of what I said. Of me. I'd scared her. She wouldn't be my ally. Whatever they'd told her about me, she'd believed it. I didn't know if I was a criminal or a lunatic in her eyes, but I couldn't be trusted. As the door shut behind her, I went to it half-heartedly. *Locked.* I had to be sure. I managed to make it back to the bed before my legs gave out.

Dread broke over me in cold waves. I'd faced death before. I thought I was prepared to face it again, but this wasn't simply about me. I loved my child. I would do anything to protect him, even give my own life. But the baby didn't stand a chance here. They knew about his heart condition and they'd taken me anyway. Why go to the trouble of pretending to care if he lived or died?

And then it hit me. This wasn't about me. It was about the baby. It had to be. Who would take the child of a king? This wasn't the work of a mad man. I knew what that looked like—chaos and blood and death. I'd seen it spread crimson on the tiles of Westminster Abbey. It was violence and insanity. It was missing the mark but hitting another.

This? It was precise and planned. It reached it into my life and pulled strings until we'd taken our proper places. This was the work of something else: hatred or greed or power.

Maybe the doctor would be willing to talk. He had my chart. He had to know the truth. When the door finally opened, I was glad I didn't have anything in my stomach or I would have thrown up.

Because the doctor did know the truth. He'd known for some time, but did I?

"Clara," Doctor Rolland greeted me. He looked as

though he'd just strolled in to my doctor's office rather than some secret torture clinic. "How are you feeling?"

He strolled into the exam room, checking the file he'd carried inside. I'd trusted this man. He was the one who had confirmed the baby's diagnosis. He'd acted concerned. He had advised me to tell Alexander the truth. To what end?

"How can you ask me that?" I spat back at him. How could he stand there and casually thumb through my paperwork? "What is this? Are you a part of this?"

"I'm a contractor. I don't ask questions, especially ones with answers I might not like. I understand this must be difficult for you," he said, "but I am a physician and I adhere to the Hippocratic oath like everyone else in my profession."

I doubted that very much. "Then you'll tell my husband where I am. You'll tell him that I've been taken."

"My patient is the baby," Rolland stopped me. "I'm here to oversee his safe delivery."

"His?" I repeated weakly.

"It's a boy." Rolland nodded, stealing the joy of knowing I'd been right. "I realize you wanted to keep it a surprise, but you may as well find out now."

"What are they going to do to the baby?" I asked softly.

"He'll be well-cared for, I promise. But there are issues that could complicate his birth. Your tests show elevated protein in your urine. The nurses will be monitoring your blood pressure for signs of pre-eclampsia." He took a seat on a nearby stool and abandoned the chart to finally look at me. His forehead was creased and worn, his eyes gentle—he was either doing a remarkable job of playing the concerned doctor or he truly was. I wasn't entirely sure if it mattered which was the truth.

"What does that mean?" If he was here to care for the baby that was all that really mattered. I would focus on that even if what I really wanted was to find the nearest sharp object and stab him in the throat.

This was as close to an ally as I would find here. I allowed the realization to slowly sink in. So long as I was pregnant, we would both be safe and cared for, but after?

"Pre-eclampsia can happen later in pregnancy, particularly high risk pregnancies. We'll need to monitor your blood pressure and watch for other signs. For instance, if your ring starts to feel tight or you begin to notice swelling." He pointed to my wedding band and I covered it with my hand.

It was still mine. It was proof that I was who I said I was. I'd forgotten it earlier. Now it stood for more than my marriage vows. It stood between life and death. I twisted it nervously around my finger. Was it tighter than it had been a few days ago? "And if this gets worse?"

"It simply means it could be time for you to have the baby." He delivered this bombshell like a bouquet of flowers.

My mouth fell open as a dozen reasons why I couldn't have the baby swam in my overrun brain. "I still have four weeks."

We were safe as long as I was pregnant. I could protect him. And I couldn't have him without Alexander by my side. He needed time. I knew he was looking to find me—to find us. By now, Georgia and Smith and everyone would be tracking us down. I needed time, and now it felt like I was on the clock.

"The baby is viable at this age and will likely do fine if we need to deliver. We'll monitor the situation," he continued. "My concern is the health of the fetus."

I almost couldn't bring myself to ask the one thing I needed to know. I'd been cut out of this equation. He'd made it clear that he was here for my son not for me. But regardless of what he said, I had to hope that he still felt some duty to me. "And the health of its mother?"

Rolland turned away and didn't answer, but the look said enough. He'd save the baby, but me?

The nurse's words earlier echoed through me: *No one is going to hurt **your** baby.*

No one would hurt either of us. I wouldn't let them.

CHAPTER 8

ALEXANDER

Clara stretched across the bed, her slender arms tied over her head. She was a work of art that I would never tire of worshipping. I wanted my mouth on her, my skin against hers, my cock buried inside her. Crawling over, she arched off the bed, trying to make contact. It seemed she had similar thoughts. Catching her nipple between my lips, I tugged it between my teeth, earning a hiss of pleasure. Every sound she made was music—my own private symphony.

"Does my poppet like that?" I asked, my hand snaking down to discover the damp heat between her thighs. "You've gotten so wet."

I plunged a finger lazily inside her, relishing how she contracted around it. She was always ready. It made it impossible to resist her, even when I was angry with her—and I was angry. I just couldn't remember why.

Clara bucked against the rope, but it held her. I'd made

certain to tie it to the bedpost so I could take my time torturing her.

"Yes, please," she whimpered.

I loved the way she circled her hips against me, trying to make contact, trying to relieve the steady need building inside her. It was a need only I could satisfy and I took not only pleasure in that but relief. In my world, there was only her. She'd been made for me. I would never understand it. I had before, and I would never do so again. "You're so greedy. You want my hands and my mouth"—I brushed a kiss over her pebbled nipple—"and my cock."

"X," she panted, craning her head, trying to raise her face to mine. "Please."

There was a desperation in her plea that settled onto my shoulders. But was I enough for her? Had I given her everything she wanted? Could I ever deserve her?

"Patience," I soothed her. "I'll give you want you need —what you've been asking for."

Running a hand over her flat belly, I paused. Something was wrong.

"What is it?" she asked.

"I don't know. I can't remember," I admitted quietly.

"Then don't stop," she urged me.

I shook my head, trying to clear the unease and concentrated on the smoothness of her skin, the freckles dusting her shoulder. Covering her mouth with mine, I stole a kiss. But it wasn't theft. Not anymore. She belonged to me. We'd given ourselves to each other.

She needed to trust me. After all this time, it was still so hard for her to do that. Maybe I needed to remind her exactly who her body belonged to—a lesson I was sure she would enjoy.

"Greedy little poppet. Greedy little cunt. I think I'll teach you how to be patient." Reaching overhead I found a second length of rope. I'd left it there, but I couldn't remember why. Now I understood.

I slid it roughly under her torso, knowing it would scratch and burn and knowing Clara wanted that. She was delicate but strong and when I treated her roughly, she became herself fully. I looped the rope around her, dragging it across her breasts. "I think these need more attention."

Clara bit her lip with each slide and tuck of the rope, gasping as I tightened it around each breast until they were plump and bound. Sitting back on my heels, I admired her. Her breasts were full and swollen from the tightness of the rope. Her fingers, while free, coiled around her restraints. Not only was she beautiful with her porcelain skin wrapped with red rope, she was where I wanted her: under my control.

"Now if I do this..." I flicked my tongue over the furl of her nipple and she yelped. "I love when you cry out like that."

"You love to see me in pain," she said without a hint of accusation. It's what she thought. It's what she believed. But she didn't understand. It was more than that.

"No, I love to see you free," I corrected her gently. "There is beauty in restraint. You look so beautiful now—so fuckable."

"Yes, please." She bit her lip and attempted to nod.

"I'm not sure." I closed my mouth over her breast again and she groaned. I could feel her grow wetter between her legs. She loved to give herself to me, but there were other considerations. "What about the baby?"

"Baby?" she repeated with a bark of laughter that marred the scene. "X, there's only you and me, remember? Us. Forever."

There was a ghost in her eyes as she spoke even though she laughed. She didn't mean it. Some part of it was a lie.

I moved my hand down her flat, unmarred stomach. We'd agreed. Just us. That was right.

Wasn't it?

"What do you want?" I turned my attention back to her. She was my world. I'd given up everything for her and received more than I could ever want. I'd never wanted that life anyway. I wanted her life.

"Take control. Do what you've always wanted to do," she breathed.

I slipped between her legs, my hands settling at her throat.

"Yes," she said with a smile as my fingers coiled around her slender neck.

My hands tightened as I thrust inside her. The smile remained as she gasped against my hold. I squeezed harder until no sound came but her body began to tremble under mine. It was what she needed—to give me total control. It was what only I could give her: protection and freedom. The knowledge rocketed through me and I filled her, watching her eyes glaze over with ecstasy until I collapsed against her. Bringing my lips to hers, I kissed her.

"Clara?" I murmured. "I love you."

She was silent. I pulled back to discover her face still washed with bliss.

Peaceful.

Free.

I'd released her. For a moment, pure joy filled me and then, when she didn't blink...

"Clara!" I bolted up in my seat, my hands reaching out and finding only air.

I'd killed her. All I'd ever wanted was to love her, and *I* had killed her.

"Alexander," Georgia called, and I turned still caught between the dream and the real world.

"I killed her," I whispered.

"There's no reason to think—"

"In the dream," I told him. "Maybe in life, too." My voice broke on the truth of it. When we met I'd warned Clara that nothing good survived around me. I'd let myself believe that might not be true. But that was a lie. It had always been a lie. Why else had I hidden so many of my family's ugly secrets? Because I'd needed to believe those lies myself.

We were tainted—infected—and I was the heart of the disease. I didn't know how to be honest. I didn't know how to be King. I didn't know how to save her. I let this happen.

"We're going to find her." Georgia came to the edge of my desk and perched against it. "Clara is a fighter. She's going to be fine."

I didn't know which one of us needed to believe that more.

"Everything is slipping away. The tighter I try to hold onto something..." My thoughts turned to my dream: to my greatest fear. I'd held so tightly to Clara that I'd finally lost her—and I had no one to blame but myself.

If I'd been honest with her from the beginning, would any of this had happened? Would my wife be sleeping in our bed?

I buried my head in my hands, trying to remind myself that I couldn't do anything about the past. I could only move forward. Wherever she was, she needed me and I wouldn't fail her. Not again.

"I don't know how to do this," I admitted to Georgia. "I'm going crazy and I need to keep my head straight. If I don't...if I don't..."

I couldn't bring myself to consider what would happen if I couldn't do that.

"Do you need to take back control?" she asked quietly.

A minute ticked by as this sank in, and we stared at one another. It was a dangerous game to play—and a more dangerous offer to make.

"What does that mean?" I asked icily.

"You're a dominant. You may need to consider whether—"

"I'm not interested," I cut her off. I wouldn't touch another woman in any capacity.

"I'm not offering," Georgia clarified. "I know you and Clara have submission all twisted up with love, but you need to consider how to keep your head clear. You need to be able to think. If that means—"

"Now isn't the time for whips," I spat out.

"It's probably the perfect time," she disagreed.

"I don't want to punish someone," I roared. How could she not see that? "I want to be punished. I want to carry her pain, because I know she's in it. I want to bear this burden."

Georgia arched a dark eyebrow. "Then hand someone else the whip."

"I thought you weren't offering." I shook my head. "I'm not interesting. Judge my marriage all you want."

"I'm not judging your marriage," she said harshly. "I'm pointing out that there's a way to clear your head and you may need to consider that option."

"And let me be clear, it's not an option." I couldn't believe she was suggesting it.

"Smith could do it," she said, ignoring me. "He knows how to separate the two. If you need punishment—if you need to step outside yourself for a moment."

"I'll keep that in mind." I wasn't about to hand anyone control over me. No matter what she thought. Even if part of me missed the vibration of a whip against my palm. Even if part of me wanted to feel its sting against my back. And the last person I would ever hand control was Smith. I respected him, but I would never bow before him. Just as no one would bow before me.

There was only one soul I knelt before, and only she could free me from this hell.

Georgia and I were both wrong. I didn't need to seek punishment. I was being punished already.

. . .

"You slept." Smith noted. He sounded oddly pleased, as if he'd been worried.

I nodded, dismissing his relief. It didn't matter that it was in a chair in my office. What mattered was that I'd wasted time. I could buy anything but that. "Don't remind me."

"You have to sleep," he said. Had he talked with Georgia? Were the two of them going to continue to mother me?

"I *have* to find her." Why was everyone else so focused on things that didn't involve bringing Clara home? She was the only thing I truly needed.

Smith didn't pursue the argument I was angling for. Instead, he shrugged. "Are you sure about this?"

I nodded again, relieved to be back on track. We'd decided the next logical course was to speak to Oliver Jacobson. Whatever this contingency was, he knew about it. We were all certain of that. He'd been a key component in too many family tragedies and he'd made his threat clear before: he'd destroy my family from within. What better way to upset the game than to steal the Queen?

Plus, since our only lead on MI-18 was missing. It was the most we had to go on. Maybe he could lead us to them.

Maybe he could lead us to her.

Something deep within me told me that Jacobson had played his part. I'd once believed he was the one pulling the strings, now I saw the ones attached to him.

We came upon Edward in the hall. He looked like it was any other day of the week—his curly hair tamed and tucked behind his ears, his navy suit pressed with crisp lines. But I saw beyond that to the circles rimming his eyes and the hollow defeat reflected there. He wasn't sleeping either.

"What are you doing here?" I asked him, sounding more accusatory then I meant to. It was my call to ask him to stay away. I wanted to protect him from this, but there was no way to shield him from the pain of losing his best friend.

"Press conference," he said flatly. He whipped his glasses off and inspected the lenses. "I wanted to avoid it, but we need to make a statement about Mary. It's been two days."

"I should handle that." I'd let it fall through the cracks. What would it look like if I was absent from this? Especially if the doctors continued their investigations into the drugs my grandmother had been taking? It was my responsibility to be the face of this family, but I'd yoked my brother with that burden.

"I've taken care of that," he explained. "We're announcing that Clara has been placed on bed rest. I've spoken with her doctor and explained that the Queen needs rest."

I let this news sink in. He'd taken care of everything. He'd stepped in and taken control of my responsibilities.

"I hope that's okay," he added quickly, misreading my silence.

I pulled my brother into a tight hug. I didn't have to do all of this. I had people I could trust, even when I was missing the ones closest to me. "Thank you."

"I've got this," he promised. "You worry about her."

"Mary's doctors want to speak to her," I reminded him.

"Bed rest," he said again. "The baby is the most important thing."

"Henry isn't going to like that."

"Henry can deal." Edward slid his glasses back on and
gave me a pointed look.

"You should check on Sarah." One of us needed to.

"I already did. She's holed up in her apartment. She
blames herself, you know."

That made two of us. It was why I hadn't visited her.

"She should be reminded that it isn't," Edward pushed.

"I'll talk to her," I promised, "later."

"And you should see your daughter," Edward added
softly. "She's asking for you."

"I will. I just—"

"She's asking for Clara," he cut me off, his Adam's
apple sliding on this revelation. "She doesn't understand."

"What am I going to tell her?" I asked him, knowing
there was no good answer for her. For any of us.

"That you love her," Edward suggested. "She may want
her mother, but she needs her father."

I thought about this for a moment. He was right. I'd
been avoiding Elizabeth for a lot of reasons. They all led
back to the same harsh reality: I'd failed her as much as I'd
failed Clara.

"Belle's taken over for Penny. Less questions," Edward
informed me.

And someone we both trusted. "Good."

"Do I want to know where you're going?" Edward eyed
Smith, who was studiously staying out of earshot.

"No."

He clapped a hand on my shoulder, one last sign of solidarity. Then heaved a sigh. I hated putting him in this position. Edward had always been the fun one, the charismatic one. Now he'd been saddled with holding up the family in the public eye. I reminded myself that if it was true—if Clara was on bed rest—he would have done the same. He would have stepped up. Because that's what family did for each other.

"We need to step in the war room," Smith said when I finally rejoined him. "Make sure we're on the same page."

Smith had persuaded me to tell the others about MI-18, a decision that rested heavily on me. I didn't know enough about the black ops department to know what would happen if we found them. Norris had warned me never to speak of the organisation leaving little room for interpretation about the possible consequences. Consequences I was choosing to ignore now. Without Norris here, I didn't have any other choices.

When we reached the meeting room, photographs lined the bulletin board on the far side of the room. Brex had been busy.

"What's this?" I asked.

He shrugged, giving me a tired grin that didn't reach his brown eyes. "You asked me to track down a covert government agency."

"And you found them?" None of the photos looked like people who would belong to a black ops unit.

"It's important to remember that covert agencies don't function with super spies alone," Georgia said dryly.

"So we started there," Brex added. "And we had something to go on. We know Norris was MI-18, so I dug into his file."

"And?" The man had been my confidant, my protector, practically my father, for my entire life. Did I want to know what they'd found?

"That's where things get interesting." He looked at Georgia for encouragement. I wasn't going to like whatever came next. "There is no James Norris. Not really. He exists on paper, but none of his background checks out."

I clutched the edge of the table so hard I thought it might splinter under my grip. "I don't understand."

"His history is made up. How much do you know about his childhood? His education?" Georgia asked me. She didn't seem nearly as nervous about this as her partner.

"Very little," I admitted. "Are you telling me he made it up?" Norris was our only connection to MI-18. I knew about the organisation because of him. It might have been easier to question if DeAngelo hadn't pointed us in the same direction.

"No. The opposite," Brex said swiftly. "We think it's all been erased so well—his life, his youth— that even he doesn't think about it anymore. He never talked about it."

Georgia nodded in agreement. "To any of us. Even I talk about my childhood."

I could only imagine the twisted, fucked-up memories she had to share. But she was right. Norris, who was full of advice and wisdom, never relied on his own past for any of it. "How does this help us?"

"We started looking for others like him," Brex continued. "Men and women with military experience and cookie cutter backgrounds."

"You found more?" I guessed, finally releasing the table. This was something. I could feel it.

"Not exactly. We found something else. Disappearances. Most labeled 'probable suicides.'"

"Probable?" I repeated.

"Sometimes there were notes, but never bodies," Georgia said.

"Why not just erase them entirely?" Smith asked. He'd been listening up until now, taking all this in with that shrewd, unnerving manner of his.

"Family. Friends. These are real people—or, at least, some of them are—and we suspect that most of them aren't dead at all."

"They're operatives," Georgia added.

"But which ones?" Smith asked.

"That's what we're trying to figure out. I've started conducting interviews with family members. Told them it was a routine follow-up to assess mental health concerns for surviving family of deceased military." Brex shrugged. If lying to grieving families bothered him, he didn't show any sign of it. Then again, if we were right, their family members were traitors. "I've only managed to speak to a half dozen, but I've heard the same thing a number of times. A few told me that they could have sworn they'd seen their loved ones. At a shop. On the street. In a park. They thought they were seeing ghosts, but..."

"You can't erase family," I muttered. If this were true, if these men and women had walked away from their lives, that didn't mean they could stay away from the people they loved, even if it was only to check in on them.

"Won't reaching out to the families be suspicious?" Smith asked. "It might be noticed."

A feline smile carved across Georgia's face. "We're counting on it."

CHAPTER 9

CLARA

I didn't want to go back to my room. I didn't want to blindly accept whatever fate these people had in store for me or my son. There were too many of them for this building to be as secure as I'd initially thought. So I took a page out of their playbook. They'd created a distraction to get to me. When June came to take me back to my 'quarters,' I took a few steps outside the exam room before I slumped against the wall.

"Oh dear!" She rushed to help me. Her arms wrapping protectively around my shoulder. I wanted to push her away, but I needed her to buy into my act.

"Sorry," I murmured, pressing a hand to my forehead. "I feel dizzy."

"You need to eat. That blood draw," she clucked. "Two days without food. Here."

Two days. Now I knew something else. I'd disappeared two days ago. I knew Alexander was searching for me. I knew he wouldn't rest, and I could only hope that two days wouldn't turn into three.

June helped me to a chair, casting pitying glances my way. "I'll be right back. Guard, can you come here!"

She waved a man over to stay with me. I knew she wouldn't trust me to stay here alone, but the guard she left me with looked me over, a mildly uncomfortable expression on his face. Was it because I was pregnant? Or because he knew who I was? I didn't care. Either way he was damned in my book. I counted down from fifty. I needed enough time to make it look real and more time to do what I needed to before she got back.

"Excuse me, I need to use the loo," I called to him.

"You can wait," he said.

"You've obviously not spent a lot of time around pregnant women," I said flatly. "Fine. Someone else will clean it up."

I was absolutely willing to call his bluff on this.

He looked torn, which meant that he would be the one who had to clean it up. His prisoner. His mess. "Fine. This way."

He clutched my arm as he led me to a bathroom, but he was surprisingly gentle. I wanted to ask him if he knew who I was, but I didn't need another unnerving, out-of-body experience.

"I'll be out here," he said.

The bathroom didn't offer any escape options, which wasn't shocking. There was a ventilation grate that I might have fit into if I wasn't carrying the equivalent of a watermelon around my torso. That was it. This place wasn't big on natural light it seemed. Being alone gave me time to think, however. They'd bring me back to the clinic. I knew that, so the most I could hope for was seeing as much of the space as possible. Information was power.

I collected myself for a moment, tucking away as much as I could: how many exam rooms we'd passed, the laboratory, the basic layout of everywhere I'd been taken. It wasn't much but it was a start. When I opened the door, I clung to it, trying to look unsteady on my feet. It was a smart move, because June was standing next to the guard holding a bowl of gelatin.

Yeah, *that* was going to do the trick.

"Thank you," I enthused, layering on the sugar. I reached out for help and the guard supported me. My fingers itched near his badge but taking it now wouldn't help me. It would be noticed before I had a chance to use it and it wouldn't take much to figure out where it had gone.

No, I needed to be smart about this. I needed a plan. I needed as much information as possible. I needed more time. I just wasn't sure how much more I had.

"Just a little something," June said, holding out a spoonful. "They'll deliver your trays later."

I wanted to gag as I swallowed, hating myself for taking her help while hating how grateful I was to have something to eat. "I appreciate it."

"Of course, dear." And she patted my hand again.

· · ·

My skin crawled wherever I'd been touched: where the nurse had held my arm while drawing blood, where the doctors hands had felt my abdomen to determine the baby's position, where June had patted my hand like she could comfort me. We returned to the dark corridor but instead of being taken to the room where I'd found the clothes, I was brought to the room next door.

"They finally have your room ready and there's fresh maternity clothes there," June told me, like she expected a reward for her thoughtfulness. I forced a smile. "I think your arrival surprised them."

How? They'd been planning this. I couldn't even imagine for how long.

"Whose room was that?" But I had a few questions for my doting nurse.

June looked to where I pointed. "Oh. That's Rachel's room."

"Rachel?" I asked. Maybe I hadn't seen a ghost after all.

"Another psychiatric case. You probably won't see her. She tends to hide."

My blood froze in my veins. *Another?* Is that what she thought I was? Was that the lie they were selling the clueless people who worked here? People who must see as little of the outside world as their prisoners?

"But her room was unlocked." It didn't make sense. Why had I been able to get to her.

"Our patients are free to roam this wing," she explained

"All the other doors were locked."

"You're free to lock yours."

Only because they could unlock it when the wanted, I was sure. "Are there many others?"

"Not now. We recently had one of our patients leave us," June smiled sadly. "Such a bright girl. I do hope she's doing well."

I did, too. I hoped she was actually free. I hoped she was telling her story to anyone who would listen and I hoped that information got back to my husband.

Most of all, I hoped that, whoever she was, she was alive.

"The loo?" I asked. I hated asking. I hated pretending that this was normal. I wasn't a patient. This wasn't a hospital. I'd been stolen—my life had been stolen.

"Down the hall, last door on the right. It locks, too," she reassured me.

So maybe that was where this Rachel was hiding unless she'd gone back to her room.

My room was about as homey as Rachel's it turned out. A bed. A shelf with a few worn paperbacks of movies I'd already seen. A dresser with some nondescript items that looked more like tents than clothing. I changed into one, grateful to cover myself despite the scratchy, ill-fitting fabric.

Not long after June disappeared, a guard showed up carrying two trays of food. He placed it in front of me without a word. Was that how they justified what they were doing? Avoiding eye contact? Not speaking to us?

As soon as he was gone, I peeked out of my room. Rachel's door was open. Grabbing the apple, I tiptoed over to it, but the room was empty and her tray untouched.

Going down the hall I discovered the loo was still locked, too. Apparently, she was more scared of me than anyone else.

"Can I use that?" I called. "I'm pregnant."

I waited, wondering if playing that card would get me enough sympathy, to lure her out. After a few seconds, I heard a lock click. Two dark eyes peeked out at me from the cracked door.

"Rachel?" I asked.

She bobbed her head.

"Dinner's here," I said. I was lying about the loo. Usually, I needed it every ten minutes, but with so little food and water, I didn't feel the urge. It was a truth that didn't sit well with me. "I thought you would want to know."

I half expected her to run back to her room and lock the door. Instead, she walked alongside me, her eyes darting nervously over her shoulder. She looked so familiar, I could swear that we'd met before, but we couldn't have. Dark eyes, long black hair that hadn't been cut in months. Years? Her skin was pale, and she was thin. Too thin. Her gait was stilted and plodding as though walking was difficult for her. It took everything in me not to start asking questions—or jumping to conclusions.

I needed her to trust me. We were in this together and I was betting that she was no more a psychiatric case than I was. But why was she here? Where had I seen her before?

"Can I eat with you?" I asked. Her room had a table. Mine only had a bed. I tried not to think what not warranting a table said about my longterm prospects for survival.

"Okay," she softly, sounding like she was trying out the word. Did she leave her often? Was that why she was skittish, because she rarely saw people?

We ate a few bites in heavy silence. It occurred to me that the food might be poisoned but I was too hungry to care. Dr. Rolland had assured me that the baby wouldn't be harmed, so for now I had to trust that. Neither of us would make it long without food anyway. When I reached for the apple I'd stashed in my pocket, she shook her head. Her hand darted out and knocked it to the floor.

"Don't eat that," she whispered, her eyes flickering around the room. "It puts you to sleep."

"An apple?" I stared at it lying on the ground.

"When I ate them, I woke up in bed but there was always something different." She pointed to her head. "My hair would be shorter or there were bruises on my arms. The last time I ate one, I woke up somewhere strange with people all around me before I fell back asleep."

What were they doing to her while she slept? What would they do to me? An icy finger ran up my spine as I remembered what Rolland had said about the baby being viable. Was that their plan? Put me into a never-ending sleep?

Rachel's eyes narrowed and she studied me for a second. "Do I know you?"

"Not sure." I reached down and pocketed the apple again. They didn't need to know I hadn't eaten it.

"How did you get here?" I asked her when I couldn't stand waiting any longer. I needed answers. Rachel didn't seem like a valuable source of information, particularly if she'd been asleep for most of their procedures, but she'd been her longer than I had. She knew things, like the bit about the apple. She could still help me.

She shrugged, her dark eyes a little glossy.

"You don't know?" I pressed. "What about your life before?"

"I remember stuff, but the doctors say I'm wrong." She sighed and I knew then that she'd given up. That was the difference between us. I wouldn't give up not until they killed me.

"What kind of stuff?" I asked. There had to be more to it.

"Crazy stuff," she whispered like she was scared they were listening in on us. In fairness, they probably were. "They told me that when I stop believing the crazy stuff I can go."

So, that's why she was so quiet. But would that work? If she just said whatever lies they sold her, they would let her go. I wished I'd been offered that deal. "How long have you been here?"

"A couple of months," she said, tacking on, "I think."

"You know, Rachel," I lowered my voice. "I remember crazy stuff, too."

"You do?" Her eyes went wild for a moment.

I seized on this sudden display of life. "I might believe you."

She shook her head, the life fading from her as quickly as it had ignited. "I want to stop believing it."

She wanted to leave. I couldn't blame her there.

"That's what he tells me to do," she continued.

"He?"

"The nice one," she says. "He comes sometimes with the guards. I don't think he's a doctor though."

"What's his name?" I asked. There had to be something else. Something more.

"Don't know." She tore a bite of bread off with her teeth. "They call him "your highness."

I went utterly still. I could have sworn my heart stopped beating. June said she didn't know who I was, but it couldn't be a coincidence that this man was called by that nickname.

"But it's like a joke. I asked him and he said they were being stupid. I don't know his name. He tells me that when I stop remembering the crazy stuff, they'll let me go," she prattled on. I didn't know if it was the food or the conversation invigorating her. I, on the other hand, felt more drained and powerless than ever.

"Okay," I said, grasping for some way to get her to tell me more. "But maybe if we think the same crazy stuff it would prove that it's not crazy. We couldn't both have gotten here the same way, right? That would mean we're not crazy."

I spoke quickly, hoping she didn't think that through too hard. It didn't begin to make sense, which meant I was really good at playing mental myself or I was finally beginning to crack.

"I guess," she said. Her nose wrinkled as if she was trying to think through my logic and get to the same conclusion. Thankfully, she must have decided the suggestion had some merit. "I was a nurse, I think. The doctors said that part is true. They say I lost a patient and had a psychotic break."

She spoke as though she was reading off a list not going from memory. It was a lie. It was painfully obvious. But why convince her she'd lost her mind? Why bring her here in the first place?

"What do you remember?" I asked her softly, unsure she would continue.

She looked over my shoulder towards a past she could still remember but no longer trusted. "I had a job. It was new and I had to sign a lot of papers. The patient was someone important, but I wouldn't find out who until I was trained."

"And?" A pit was opening in my chest as she continued —as I began to understand what had happened.

"I showed up at the job. It was on a private estate. That's it. Then I woke up. Something must have happened to the patient. That must have been when I had the psychotic break." For some reason, arriving to this thought seemed to please her.

She'd begun to buy their story, but how long had they been selling it to her? Was that the fate that actually awaited me? Not death, but rather a gradual slipping away of everything that made me who I was—of everything I loved.

They say that there's always some truth needed to sell a

lie. And this mystery patient? I had a terrible feeling that was real.

Too many things were falling into place. I stared at her again. "You never saw the patient?"

She lifted her thin shoulders before letting them slump back to their previously defeated position. "I don't remember."

"The house?" I said desperately. I needed to know, even if I didn't want to. "Do you remember where it was?"

"I shouldn't say," she whispered. "The documents said I couldn't."

Even after all this time, she was doing her job. If only she realized the truth, maybe she wouldn't feel beholden to those agreements any longer.

I lowered my voice to match hers. "It's important."

"It belonged to the royal family," she said her voice so quiet now that I hoped I was hearing things.

But I wasn't.

The royal family. The house belonged to us—and there was a house and a patient. But why? Why drug a nurse? Why lock her away? What did she see that warranted such a cruel punishment?

Unless...

I had to know if I was crazy or if I'd finally found a piece to a puzzle I didn't know I was solving. There was one way to do it.

"Rachel, do you have any idea who I am?" I asked in a strangled voice.

She shook her head, studying me for a moment like she might find a clue. "Should I?"

"No." I said. There was one more question that would tell me everything I needed to know, one that could raise a million others. I asked anyway. "What year is it?"

She cocked her head looking at me like I was the crazy one. "2009."

CHAPTER 10

It hadn't taken him long to figure out exactly where he was—that was the first and last bit of good news.

The nurse believed he knew where the Queen was, which meant she was still missing. He didn't know what category to sort that info into. It didn't quite add up—the attack, the interrogation, the restraints binding him now—which was how he knew it was all a lie.

Alexander had not sent him here. He wasn't under suspicion from anyone. That was how it worked, though.

It was how they broke people.

It was how he'd been trained to break people.

They seemed to have forgotten that very important point. Whatever tactic they'd tried next would be equally transparent.

Then again, maybe that was the point. Sometimes, wasting time was simply that. The more time he spent trying to figure out what they were up to, the more time they had to enact whatever scheme they'd been plotting.

He hadn't wanted to believe that it would all come back to this. He'd chosen to turn a blind eye to them and his own past. That was a mistake that would cost him. He could only hope it wouldn't cost the ones he loved most as well.

So, he'd waited until it looked like he was under, then he'd carefully regulated his heart rate enough that it did register while he broke the fingers in his right hand—all while pretending to be under sedation.

Someone had forgotten that he'd been trained to withstand most sedatives. Or maybe that they thought that was a skill he'd long forgotten. That mistake was going to cost them.

He hated resorting to his dominant hand, especially since he'd compromised his other earlier, but this was more important.

He needed to get out. He needed to find Alexander and tell him what he suspected. It was the only way Clara would be found. It was her only chance. He owed them that. He owed his true family that.

When his hand finally slipped free, he paused to consider his next steps. He had moments before the alarm went off, once he detached the monitors. That meant he had to be ready for action. He undid his other restraint and pulled the blanket over his mangled hands to hide the truth. He couldn't act. Not yet.

It was a frustrating truth that sometimes, even when time was running out, you had to wait for the right moment to strike.

CHAPTER 11

ALEXANDER

I'd promised myself that if I ever saw Oliver Jacobson as a free man, I would kill him on the spot. Now, as we made our way to Knightsbridge, I wondered if that was still an option. Oliver Jacobson might prove a valuable source of information if he ever bothered to speak in a language that wasn't riddles. In the time we kept him in custody, he hadn't given us anything other than vague threats and innuendo. But he knew more than he let on. That had become apparent to me when, while sitting in a cell, he'd admitted to the Child Watch attack. He hadn't been involved, but he'd still known it happened. Since I'd made certain he didn't so much as know the outcome of the latest Arsenal match, it was a surprise.

He knew what they were planning then, and I ventured to guess he knew what was going on now. But Jacobson wasn't going to roll over.

"He won't tell us anything," I said to my companion, voicing my thoughts.

"Leave that to me." Smith's eyes stayed on the road as he darted around bold tourists and slow cab drivers.

I appreciated his confidence, even if I didn't share it. "If he was going to crack, he would have used it to get out of prison."

"Face it, Alexander," Smith muttered, narrowly missing a lorry. "He didn't need the leverage. Whoever is behind this—truly behind this—got him out. He didn't talk, because he didn't have to talk."

"Why would he talk now?" I muttered.

"I can be persuasive," Smith promised darkly.

I had no doubt about that, but given my past with Jacobson there were other considerations. "I can't exactly walk into his house and beat the shit out of him. No matter how much I might like to."

"You aren't the only one. Trust me. But there are more persuasive methods to break a man than physical violence."

"But physical violence is the most satisfying," I grumbled. Jacobson deserved it. He'd been an integral part of the plan that had ended in my father's death. "He texted me, you know."

"He did?" Smith sounded surprised.

I hadn't shared this bit with anyone until now, and I wasn't exactly sure why. There had been important matters to consider than a vague text. I'd just discovered my wife wasn't at home. I'd just begun to panic.

My nightmare had only been beginning.

"The night she disappeared. It said 'from within.'" My hands clenched into fists as I recalled the dawning horror of that moment.

Smith shot me a quizzical look. "From within? What does that mean?"

"He said it to me once. He told me that the way to destroy the royal family was from within." I hadn't known what he meant then, but Jacobson had been right. Ripping Clara from me meant I would do anything, give up anything, to get her back. I would break any law. I would hurt, torture, kill—whatever it took to bring her safely home.

If I had to I would burn this city to the ground.

"You think that means taking Clara?" Smith asked.

"What else could it mean?" I watched him for a moment aware of how carefully he arranged his features. But he couldn't hide the darkness in his eyes. I knew that look. Something had sparked, turning the wheels in his mind, and whatever he was thinking, he wasn't sure if he should share it.

"Maybe nothing," Smith said.

"I don't have a lot else to go on," I admitted. Two days and nothing more than a bit of gossip from London's most in-the-know gangster wasn't getting us far. We had theories. Insane theories. But what I wanted was something tangible —something I could wrap my mind around.

"I need to talk to Georgia." Smith was stalling, but why?

"Tell me," I demanded.

Smith slowed the Bugatti as we came to a traffic light, but despite the stop, he didn't turn to face me. "I understand wanting something to go on, but I need to speak with her. It was something she said."

"I could order you to tell me," I warned him. I would, too. Whatever tentative alliance we'd formed, however much I'd begun to respect Smith Price, I would do whatever I had to do to get answers.

Smith smirked, raising an eyebrow. "Order me?"

"I am the King." I felt like a dick for playing that card, but it had to count for something.

"You aren't my king. I'm Scottish. You'll find my family's roots in the Jacobite rebellion," he informed me. There was a slight grin on his face as if he'd been granted a wish.

"Been waiting a long time to say that to me?" I asked.

"Nah, but I imagine my ancestors would be proud all the same." The light turned and he continued into the exclusive neighbourhood where Oliver Jacobson, supposed man of the people, lived. "Look. I don't want to turn this into a witch hunt. There's following a lead and there's causing trouble. We don't have time for trouble."

I couldn't argue with him there. We were running out of time. Clara was due in a few weeks, but the truth was that the baby could come at any time. Not knowing where she was or what was happening to her was driving me crazy. But that wasn't the most important thing. Clara's job was to protect the baby and I knew she would. It was my job to look after her, protect her, support her—and she needed me more than ever. "I only hope Norris is with her."

It was a vain hope. I couldn't imagine anyone taking Norris alive, even if part of me wanted to because the alternative was too much to bear.

"Have you ever considered—truly considered—that Norris might not—"

"I trust Norris with everything, especially my wife," I cut him off, knowing where he was going with this.

"There's a lot you don't know about Norris," Smith pointed out.

I could understand why he felt that way. I had it on good authority that his own man had betrayed him to Hammond a few years ago. But this was different. Norris was different.

"He's my family, and while we may be a fucked up bunch, I trust my family. We look out for one another. We have to," I said, my voice vibrated with suppressed annoyance. Considering Norris a suspect was a waste of time. Perhaps Smith had never known true loyalty.

Smith pulled into a vacant space in front of a row of houses and remained silent. If he had more to say on the subject, he wasn't going to share. That was good because I wasn't interested in hearing it.

"Did you bring an entourage?" Smith asked, his eyes glued to the rearview mirror.

Swiveling in my seat, I turned to discover two black Aston Martins behind us. One slid into a vacant spot, the other pulled up beside the passenger window.

"I didn't," I said in a low voice. These weren't our men, but we both recognised a security team when we saw it.

It made sense that Jacobson would increase security. Public opinion regarding his alleged participation in my father's assassination was mixed. Some people didn't believe it. Others wrote it off as the nasty business of politics. But there were a fair few that believed he was a traitor. I was one of them. Even amongst those that didn't support the monarchy there was a fair bit of horror over the allegations. It seemed whether you supported king or not, nearly everyone supported country—and the attack had been against everything Great Britain stood for.

Parliament's initial outrage over his arrest and incarceration had cooled once the matter had become a matter for public opinion. Most members had remained tight-lipped regarding the matter with very few voicing support for their colleague.

"Should I handle this?"

I blinked at Smith's question. It took me a moment to see things from his perspective. He had stepped into the role of bodyguard albeit begrudgingly. Norris would usually have handled this. It was part of our unspoken arrangement. Smith and I on the other hand weren't exactly friends, and I wasn't exactly his employer. Our relationship was something different entirely. He now fell into the category of fucked up family I'd been defending moments earlier.

That didn't make it his job to handle things now.

"We might as well do it together," I muttered, opening my car door before he could protest, but Smith didn't.

Instead he tossed me a pair of aviators. "A little extra camouflage in case we've attracted any prying eyes."

He respected my decisions in a way most members of my team didn't. He was also far less likely to take a bullet for me. In my opinion, it was the perfect balance.

Stepping out of the Bugatti, I slipped the sunglasses on,

knowing that between the stubble I'd been ignoring and my t-shirt and jeans I didn't look much like myself. Then again, reporters had a long memory. Only a few years ago, I'd looked like this often. Back when I'd first met Clara. Back when we'd moved into our place in Notting Hill. Back when our life felt impossible. A lot had changed.

A man had gotten out of each car, but left the engine running. The one closest to me inclined his head. "Your Majesty."

Jacobson might not respect me but his men did.

"You can tell him that we're here. I'm unarmed." I still hadn't bothered to get a gun despite my conversation with Smith. He was right. It would be necessary. For now, though, I was telling the truth. I shoved my hands in my pocket and waited.

The man glanced to the row of white houses behind us. "We don't represent Jacobson."

"Then we don't have any business," Smith said, stepping next to me. Unlike me, he'd found the time to use a razor and change into a suit. He looked every bit the part of a lawyer. I wondered if that was purposeful. In a way it was his own disguise, hiding the wild streak in him under a coat of civility.

"Our employers would like you to reconsider speaking with Jacobson," the man continued.

"You'll find I don't take well to orders." It was a hazard of being a king. I didn't appreciate being told what to do.

"Consider it a request from friends."

Smith and I looked to one another considering this so-called request. There weren't many people who would have the balls to surround men like us and ask a favour. That fact alone was worth considering. Another time that might have been enough, but each moment I spent not knowing where my wife was a second less than I would show those who took her.

"Unfortunately, gentleman, this is a matter of national security," I said calmly, taking a step away from the car. It was only then I realized that another man had circled round us to wait on the sidewalk.

"As is this," the man assured us. "You won't find the answers you're looking for from Oliver Jacobson. He's been effectively isolated."

I sucked in a breath as I felt that door slam shut. It had always been a long shot to get Jacobson to talk, but it had been our most promising option. We knew he was involved, even if it wasn't clear how much he actually knew about the plan. If these people had cut him off from the others involved with Clara's disappearance, they would pay for it. "On whose orders?"

I wanted to know who had cocked this up so magnificently. When Jacobson had been freed, we'd watched him closely for any signs he was in contact with others. But there'd been no activity. I'd thought it was a play to look innocent. Now that I knew the truth, I realized someone had been manipulating the situation.

"They don't have a name, but they are friends. For now," he added ominously.

That cleared it up. There was only one group who had their fingers on the pulse of this situation who would dare to step in. I'd been avoiding seeking their help.

Smith stiffened next to me, the only sign that any of this had shaken him.

"They would like to speak with you, if you would be so kind as to follow us." He didn't wait for a response instead, he circled around the black saloon and slid in.

We waited until the other did the same. They had us blocked in for the moment, but that didn't mean either of us would blindly follow.

"This could be a trap," Smith said instantly.

"I know." I ran a hand through my hair, wondering how to process all the information left unspoken during this exchange. "It's the Ghosts."

"That seems obvious, but..." he trailed away, and I knew what he wasn't saying.

Too obvious? Whoever was behind Clara's disappearance would know about the Council of Ghosts, the shadowy group that decided when a monarch needed to be deposed. They knew that any king would fear them. But I wasn't any king and I had nothing left to lose.

"If it's a trick, they'll lead us to answers," I argued. Possibly to wherever they kept Clara.

"Or they'll put a bullet in your brain," Smith said, shaking his head. "It's a risk. Why would the Council be involved with Jacobson? Or any of this?"

I smirked despite myself. That I understood without doubt. "It's all ego. Another party stepped into their territory. Whoever killed my father crossed a line."

Smith looked to number 414. The house Jacobson called home was innocuous, blending in to its surroundings just as he had, even if it was a bit too high brow for a man who railed against the aristocracy. "He's not the one we're after."

It was a realization that stung. We both had good reason for wanting to see Jacobson dead. He'd threatened our families. He'd pulled strings and ruined lives. Did it matter if he wasn't the one in charge? He was responsible for causing our loved ones pain. He had tried to take our wives from us. "He doesn't deserve to live."

"He doesn't deserve to die by a king's hand, either. That's too good a death for him. He'll think it means he was right. He should waste away," Smith said in a hollow voice. "Let him rot until everyone sees him for what he truly is."

"And them?" I asked, tipping my head to the cars idling around us.

"They might have answers," he said.

We both knew they might not. The possibility was all that mattered. We'd been grasping at shadows for days, so why not go to see the ghosts? I reached for the door handle and nodded. "It's worth it if they do."

"And if they don't?" Smith called as he went to the driver's side.

I didn't answer him. With each shut door and dead end, I felt further from Clara. She was my light. Maybe I was desperately seeking some new source of hope to tap, but I was a man caught in a labyrinth and with each failure, I learned something. Eventually, the path would be clear. I had to believe that.

I had no other choice.

.   .   .

IT WASN'T A SURPRISE WHEN WE WERE LED TO White's, but it did dispel the tension lingering in the car. This was where we'd met the council last time. Smith had been with me. I felt a hollow pang remembering Norris by my side as well. I wished he was here now, guiding me. Because even if all signs pointed to the legitimacy of this meeting, I couldn't ignore that this was a group of men who held the power of life and death over me.

Smith shot the valet a terrifying look when he held his hand out for the keys. "Worth more than your life."

The younger man's eyes widened and he nodded.

"You have a way with people," I muttered as we made our way inside. I'd kept the sunglasses on for good measure. My brother had just announced the news of our grandmother's death and that my wife was on bed rest. I didn't know how it would look to be seen going into a club.

"He didn't take one look at you," Smith said smoothly as we waited for the doorman. "No one did. You're welcome."

I snorted, only half believing that his little show had anything to do with me and everything to do with the multi-million dollar car he'd just entrusted to some pipsqueak.

Once, we were inside, we could both relax. A little. White's was a notoriously elitist club, which meant that no one here would risk their membership for a bit of gossip. The porter at the desk recognised me from our last disastrous encounter and waved us in without comment.

"I thought they might require a blood sample this time,"

Smith said flatly as we climbed the stairs. "Spent much time here in your youth?"

"My father had his man run here as soon as I was born and proved genetically entitled," I told him. "A decision I'm sure he regretted since he never once asked me to come along, and I never bothered to come on my own. Not my type of place."

Smith's lips twitched. We both knew that the types of clubs I'd preferred in my younger days had a very different atmosphere. "It reminds me of The Library."

"The Library?" I repeated.

"It's a lot like this but with more whips," he added in a low voice. "Very discreet. Should you ever…"

"I'm a married man," I said, and I would be for the rest of my life. Once Clara was back in my arms, I wouldn't need anything else. "Clara is all I want."

"She'd be welcome," he assured me. He didn't press the subject further. Perhaps sensing that talk of my wife upset me. Perhaps not wanting to remind me of her absence more.

The Cigar Club was empty save for the presence of the men believed to control my destiny: the Council of Ghosts. The last time we'd faced them, the Prime Minister had been present. Today he was absent, and in his seat was a familiar face.

CHAPTER 12

CLARA

Her face told me everything I needed to know. Since the doctor had warned me about my condition, June had come to monitor my blood pressure dutifully every few hours. I never asked her what it was. Sometimes she would smile to herself. Other times she would frown. Now her face was a collection of hard, straight lines.

Something was wrong.

And this time I couldn't keep my mouth shut.

"Is the baby okay?" I asked, nerves getting the better of me. Rubbing my stomach, I willed my little boy to stay put a while longer. At least, until mommy had a plan.

"Everything is fine." Her eyes told a different story as they darted away from my face. "The doctor is being cautious."

I wouldn't have believed her anyway.

Rachel, who had become my shadow since our heart to heart, had stayed tucked in a corner behind us while June did her examination. Close enough to see everything that was going on, but far enough not to get yelled at. She'd learned her lesson when she'd bothered to ask June a question earlier today and gotten her head ripped off. It had shown me a different side of June. Maybe the nurse believed the lies they told her. Maybe she was a really good actress. Either way, she was either choosing ignorance or too stupid to know the truth.

"How are you feeling? Are you getting enough to eat?" she asked, turning on her bedside manner like she was flipping a light switch.

It might have been soothing in another circumstance. "Does it matter?"

"We need to keep the baby healthy," June chastised me, her voice taking on a hard edge.

Of course, we did. I wanted to tell her that I'd been doing a fine job of that until I was stolen from my home and husband. But I knew how she'd pat my arm and tell me everything would be fine. She could keep trying to convince me I was crazy. I knew the truth.

But was I the only one? Had word gotten out yet? Was Alexander still looking for me? Did the rest of the world know?

The more time I spent with June, the more I suspected she knew exactly what she was doing. How couldn't she? Unless she'd lived under a rock—or in this hellhole bunker —she knew exactly who I was. She could play sweet, innocent nurse all day long and I'd pretend alongside her— while waiting for an opportunity to crush this snake with my heel.

"When will the baby come?" I asked. I already knew

we wouldn't be waiting until I went into labor. My doctor had wanted to control the baby's arrival. Dr. Rolland would want the same. But whereas Dr. Ball would have waited until I was near term, I got the impression that I was being prepped for delivery.

"Probably very soon. Ideally with a male child, we want to wait until the lungs develop, but your blood pressure seems to be a problem," she admitted.

It was the most she'd told me. I grabbed a pillow, willing myself to stay calm. This was about my blood pressure and maybe I had some control over that. It seemed unlikely given the circumstances, but I would try. It was all I could do until I finally got a chance to make a run for it.

June's eyes softened, mistaking my silence for fear. "Don't worry. A friend is coming to see you."

"A friend?" I repeated, wishing I'd heard her wrong and hoping she would correct me.

She didn't. "Before the baby comes. To check on you."

Bile rose in my throat and I forced it to stay down. I wouldn't show any weakness. Not to her. Not to them. "*My* friend?"

"I assume." She smiled warmly as she collected the blood pressure cuff and her stethoscope.

As she bustled around the room, casting annoyed glances at Rachel, dread mounted inside me. Were they going to take someone else? Bring someone here to comfort me? Why bother? Why pretend at humanity when they had none?

I couldn't even process the other possibility.

No friend of mine would be in on this.

No one I knew or loved could ever do this to me or Alexander.

But even as I told myself this, I knew it wasn't true. They wouldn't go to the trouble to take Belle or Edward simply to give me some company. I had plenty of that with Rachel hovering around my room.

I also knew one thing: whoever was coming was no friend of mine.

"I'll be back to check on you this evening," June told me, "but I need to get these to the doctor."

After she was gone, Rachel peeked out from the shadows, her swallow face equally grim.

"That bad?" I breathed. Rachel had been a nurse. She'd been paying attention to everything June had tested me for, explaining what she could. Judging from her expression, time was running out.

She nodded slowly. "Your blood pressure is really high. They'll need you to deliver the baby."

I wanted to ask her why. I wanted to know how staying pregnant could be any worse for either of us. As long as the baby was inside me, he was safer than he would ever be in their hands. But she didn't understand that. She couldn't. To her, we were two nut jobs locked up for our own good. She would trust them.

Even so, she still knew more than me. "What happens if I don't have him now?"

"You could die," she said, looking like a child facing the prospect of losing her new toy.

Part of me wanted to comfort her—to lie and say it

would all be okay. The other part of me had nothing left to give, because I had a feeling I was going to die either way.

"It's nice that a friend is coming to visit you." Rachel changed the subject in a doomed attempt to cheer me up.

"Yes," I said in a clipped tone, not wanting to shatter her illusions any more.

When she'd first spoken to me, it had taken effort to compose myself when she told me what year it was. I'd considered telling her the truth—that ten years had passed —but how could I? And would she even believe me?

It wouldn't do any good. It might push her over the edge she seemed to constantly teeter on. I doubted Rachel was insane when she came here, but this place? How could anyone survive this without losing bits of themselves?

Still, she was the only ally I had and I would use our new friendship if I had to.

"Rachel," I said, "could you help me to the bathroom?"

I needed to speak to her somewhere without cameras. I knew they were watching us now and if I was going to plead my case, I couldn't do it here.

I wasn't giving up. Somewhere I knew Alexander was looking for me. I knew he was burning down the world for me. I owed him every ounce of fight I had left.

I owed it to our child.

Rachel helped me down the hall, but when we reached the door, I motioned for her to follow me inside.

It would look suspicious, but I could lie—claim I was having another dizzy spell and needed the support. I only needed a few minutes. I had to try to convince her and not simply for my own sake, for hers. They'd stolen her life as well. She deserved to know.

"I need to talk to you," I said in a hurry. I had no doubt that we wouldn't have long before someone came to check on us if we lingered. Someone was always coming around to peek into our rooms and check the corridor. Whoever was watching the cameras would have seen us go in together.

"Okay," she said, looking frightened. Not of them, I realized. Of me.

She'd bought the lie they sold her so well that she still didn't realize she was a prisoner not a patient. It was that lie that made her more scared of me than she was of them. It worked in their favor and kept her in line.

It also made asking for her help a big gamble. But I was running out of options. If she was right about the blood pressure reading, it wouldn't be much longer. Once they took me into surgery—I didn't know if I would wake up.

"I have to get out of here," I told her. "The baby needs special medical care."

"They'll take care of the baby." She shifted on her heels, eyeing the door. I half expected her to dart for it. It was clear she didn't like being in here without anyone watching.

"They're lying to you, Rachel. You need to know the truth. You can't trust them." How could I make her see? Anything I said would be treated with suspicion. She believed I was the crazy one.

And what could I do? Tell her the truth? That ten years had passed since she was brought here? That I had no idea why they'd done this to her? Why she'd been targeted? It sounded insane, because it was. Everything about this was crazy.

No, I couldn't tell her that. She was too fragile not like glass but rather like a bomb. I had to take a different approach.

"Please. My husband and daughter need me," I begged her.

"You have another child?" This got her attention.

"A little girl. Elizabeth." I nodded, my heart aching to hold her.

"She must miss you," Rachel said softly.

Finally, I was getting somewhere. Still, what I was about to say next was a big risk. "You met my husband. Just for a moment. The day you woke up in the strange place. I was there and he was there. He came and spoke to you, remember? You asked him about your family, and he told you I was his wife."

The confusion clouding her dark eyes stormed. She remembered. The trouble was that it seemed like she didn't want to.

"Why would he let them put you in here?" she asked.

"He doesn't know where I am," I said frantically. In the hall, I heard a heavy door slam shut and footsteps on the cement. Time was up and I hadn't convinced her. "Please. If you know anyway to get out. I have to find him."

Rachel glanced between me and the door, then she lifted one finger to her lips and nodded.

"Thank you." I wanted to cry. Instead, I turned to wash

my hands. I needed to be able to sell a lie to whoever was on the way to check on us.

Rachel opened the door a crack and peeked out. When she pulled her head back in, her wide smile made the hairs on my arm stand on end. "He came!"

"Who?" My heart stuttered as I asked.

"The nice one. The one they call your highness. I told you about him," she reminded me.

She waited, obviously wanting a cue for me. But I didn't know what to do? On the other side of the door was someone I didn't want to see for who they really were. I had no doubt this was the friend June said would come. I'd thought I would have longer, but it seemed the clock was winding down.

I recalled something that Norris said to me once: love doesn't run on clocks.

I supposed that was true. When I was gone, Alexander and I's love would remain. But only he would feel it. Our daughter would hear about how I loved her but never know it.

Right now, I—my heart, my body, my life—was on a clock and I suspected the person on the other side of the door knew when that clock would stop.

It took everything in me to open that door to face the person who'd betrayed me. I wasn't certain what to expect, and when I finally opened the door, I met the wolf in friend's clothing that had betrayed us all.

CHAPTER 13

ALEXANDER

I stared at my uncle waiting for an explanation. He didn't belong here among my self-appointed conscience. Not here with these men who'd served in Parliament for decades. He wasn't one of them, and now I knew: he wasn't one of us either.

When no one spoke, I finally lost control. "What are you doing here?"

"I'm happy to explain that if you'll sit down," he said serenely, his saintly demeanor not quite matching the all black suit he'd worn.

He was in mourning.

I didn't care.

My uncle, Henry, had been a thorn in my side since he'd returned with my grandmother to reinstate the sodding Sovereign Games. Everything had been a mess since then. I'd been unable to contain the truth about Anderson Stone. Clara had taken too much interest in the games. And then, mysteriously, my wife had found herself at the bedside of my long assumed dead sister. All these problems could be traced back to Henry's arrival.

He apparently liked to be at the center of whatever new family scandal was brewing. I'd gladly let him take all the pity for my grandmother's death, but I hadn't come here to talk it over with him.

I was here for information.

"What is the meaning of obstructing my access to a known criminal?" I demanded.

Smith took a chair, at ease with letting me confront them.

"We were saving you the trouble," Clark, a member of the House of Lords with a reputation almost as auspicious as his bushy white eyebrows, informed me. "We've kept this meeting to the pertinent parties."

There was one person missing today. The Prime Minister had been present during my first meeting with the infamous Council. Clark's implication was that he wasn't a necessary party. It said something to the sway they held, but whether or not that translated into something useful in this situation.

"Then why is he here?" I asked. I had no reason not to like my uncle, but his presence was unnerving. Up until a few hours ago, we'd kept Clara's kidnapping quiet. Now more and more people I didn't well enough to trust were finding out. "I agreed to meet with you!"

"We're in the habit of conducting meetings, not yelling matches." Byrd was one of the oldest members of Parliament and of the men here the most likely to become an actual ghost the soonest. He didn't have time for any of it, not even the king, it seemed.

I waited a moment, still glowering over Henry's presence. I didn't like this. It had all the markers of a set-up. Had he weaseled his way into their good graces or had they kept his membership a secret?

"Alexander, I'm not your enemy," Henry said as though reading my mind.

Yes, but he wasn't exactly my ally either. Not if he was here amongst men who judged whether I was suitable to carry the crown or not. Since he was my family, I might have expected him to be on my side, but he was here sitting with them instead.

"Then what are you?" I dropped into a chair, my eyes glued to him like he might vanish.

"He is the dark prince," Clark informed me.

"The what?" Smith asked for me.

"The council relies on someone within the royal family to provide reliable intel on the mental well-being of the king. Henry has done so for decades. He was our link to Albert. Now he is our link to you."

That's why he'd suddenly decided to return to London. I'd begun to shake things up. I had questioned Parliamentary rights versus my rights as King. I'd blessed my brother's marriage. The Council must have been concerned about my next controversial move.

"You're a spy," I accused.

"I never share information just my assessments and opinion," Henry said, toying with the cuffs of his jacket. It was a nervous gesture that had also plagued my father.

He was uncomfortable, but why?

He could claim whatever he wished, but it didn't change the facts. "I can't say that it feels benevolent to find out a member of my family speaks to a secret council behind my back."

"It is," Henry assured me. "The dark prince is brought in as a counter measure. I see the private life. I was privy to what Albert struggled with. I saw into your home life."

"He was the one who assured us that you weren't a loose cannon," Byrd said as though this absolved Henry's actions entirely.

"Merely progressive," Clark added. Byrd's lips pursed as though he disapproved of this, but otherwise didn't speak. "Someday, another member of your family will take the role."

"Who?" I asked. There was no one in my family who would willingly take the role. Whereas Albert had maintained a slight distance between himself and everyone else in his life after my mother's death, there was no one close to me that I would push away.

"We can't share that. It's out of the ordinary to reveal this to you now."

"No one in my family will spy on me," I told them.

"You're looking at this the wrong way. The shadow royal protects the monarch. He finds justification for seemingly illogical actions. He helps guide a king back onto the right path."

"Protects?" I asked, calling their bluff. "So none of these so-called shadows have ever turned against the crown."

The monarchy had spent far too many periods at war amongst itself for such a duty to go without abuse. I could point to moments in history where I seriously doubted this *shadow royal* had protected the reigning king.

"Rarely, but it has happened," Clark admitted. "Not in the way you assume. Sometimes there is nothing defensible in a man's actions. Sometimes, it's merely the misuse of power. A shadow knows exactly which is which."

"How is that?" I didn't buy it. Any of it. "What if they simply want the crown for themselves?"

"Because the shadow knows the king on an intimate level, and they are in a position where the crown will never become theirs."

That narrowed down the possible options, but hardly seemed foolproof. I couldn't imagine who they would find to fulfill this position, but Henry definitely didn't know me on an intimate level.

"Why reveal this to me now?" What did any of this have to do with Jacobson or Clara? "What does this have to do with my situation?"

"I've tried to guide you. They know that. But I can't continue this position. You resist most counsel." Henry cleared his throat. "I find it troubling given..."

That wasn't true. I didn't know Henry well enough to trust him. I knew now that I never would.

"This has been enlightening, gentleman. But we have pressing matters." My heart was racing, blood pounding. How dare they interrupt the investigation? How dare they steal valuable time from the search for Clara? They knew what was going on. I was certain of that or they wouldn't have stepped between me and Jacobson's door.

"Jacobson does not know where your wife is nor does he have access to the men that do," Byrd said in a low voice as I pushed to my feet.

"What do you know about my wife?" I was on edge—one spark away from explosion. Everyone in the room seemed to know that, but they continued to light matches with their riddles and distractions.

"We know she's been taken," Henry said gently.

He knew. I stared at him, astonished. I wanted to know for how long. He hadn't come to me. He hadn't offered counsel or friendship or support. He'd stayed away like a goddamn coward.

"Why do you care?" I asked, flinging an accusatory finger his direction. "You told the doctors it was Clara that handled Mary's medication."

I hadn't forgotten that Henry had done nothing to help Clara in the eyes of the doctors. I hadn't forgotten the suspicion clouding his eyes after his mother's death. If he believed she was responsible, he didn't know either of us, which meant he couldn't help us now.

"I was shaken," Henry admitted, regret colouring his words, "but I know Clara would never do such a thing."

Now he spoke in her defence. Was it because of our mixed company? Or because he actually believed it?

"The matter's been dropped. We've seen to it," Clark said. "Besides that, even if she was guilty, it wouldn't be the first time a queen poisoned an in-law."

They spoke as if such behaviour was forgivable.

Perhaps the Council of Ghosts were more modern than they appeared. Or perhaps, monarchs could get away with murder. If so, I had a few people I wouldn't mind deposing.

"Someone did have access to her medication," Henry said, "and we should find out who."

"The staff?" Smith offered.

Given how many people had access to our private rooms and saw to our needs, it was a good guess. Even with all our security protocols, it was possible someone had slipped through.

"Too obvious," Clark said. "We screen all the individuals working in the palaces."

"I thought that was our job," Smith said dryly. I couldn't help but note how willingly he'd accepted his role on my team. Perhaps, this wasn't temporary assistance, after all.

"We have slightly different criteria," Byrd said.

In other words, they wanted to make sure someone didn't step on their toes. If someone was going to off the King, it was them. So then how had they missed this?

"If it's not the staff..." I spread my hands not sure where this left us.

"Then it's family or friends."

"My grandmother didn't have friends," I said flatly, earning a sharp look from Henry. "It's true. Not even you could stand her."

"We weren't speaking of her friends and family. We were speaking of yours," Clark clarified.

Smith's left eyebrow shot up and he dared a look at me as if to say *are they suggesting what I think they are?* He'd questioned the loyalty of those surrounding me and knew how I felt on the matter.

"I trust those closest to me with my life." This statement was met by a shared look of apprehension that tightened my already stretched nerves.

What else did they know?

I couldn't stand the constant doubt that simmered around them. Why tread like we were walking among landmines when someone had a gun to our heads? Now was the time for action, not hesitation.

"Perhaps, you shouldn't trust them all," Henry suggested gently.

"I suppose I should reconsider," I said, glaring at him. I'd never trusted Henry— not truly. But I'd never let him near me. He'd been close to Clara. Too close. "It was you, wasn't it? You told her about Sarah."

Henry nodded, a pained expression shuddering his eyes for a moment. "I pointed her in a direction. Secrets destroy marriages. I saw that too clearly with your father and mother."

I wasn't buying his remorseful act. "My father was no saint."

"Neither was your mother," Henry said pointedly. "They were both simply humans."

I wanted to ask him what he meant by that. I wanted to ask him how he dared to pretend he was part of this family while he was playing both sides. I wanted to tell him that he'd nearly cost me my marriage.

But that wasn't true. I had nearly cost me my marriage. It was a sobering thought, but not nearly as disturbing as the thought that followed. Even now having done every-thing right, I might have lost Clara anyway.

"We should stay on track," Smith suggested, calling my attention back to the threats.

"Unless you have answers about my wife, this is wasting my time." I nodded once to the Council, the most deference I would show any of them. They might be King-makers but I already wore the crown.

Byrd's mouth turned down. Of all the men who sat judging me, I disappointed him the most. It was like having my father in the room.

"We believe you are looking in the right direction regarding certain *nonexistent* agencies," Clark said, finally circling round to the reason I'd come.

"How comforting coming from a *nonexistent* council," I muttered. It was too little too late. I'd run out of time for listening to a board of sphinxes. "Thank you for the pat on the back. We need to go."

They'd saved me the time of speaking with Oliver Jacobson and possibly the trouble of cleaning up a mess if I couldn't keep my hands off of him. I suppose I owed them for that. But if they expected a thank you for wasting my time, they had another thing coming.

They'd interrupted this sordid game I'd been caught in mid-play. I had no idea what that would cost me. If they'd given our enemies time to move, it might be a price I would extract from them.

"If MI-18 is active, you should tread carefully," Byrd advised. "They are no friend of either this government or your family."

This was actually useful, a fact I found surprising.

"Then who are they looking out for?" I asked darkly. Part of me had wondered if MI-18 answered to them. They seemed to have enough men in play. But if MI-18 wasn't controlled by the people or the crown that made them more dangerous than we'd guessed.

Until this moment, hadn't been certain if we were searching for an ally or an enemy. Part of me had hoped, given Norris's background with the organisation, they might help us. According to the Ghosts, they might be the ones behind this.

"That's a question we must ask ourselves, and I believe it's best to start with your ties to them," Clark said.

I bit my lip. I wouldn't reveal Norris to them or that he was missing, although I suspected that was what they were insinuating. "We have no ties."

"That's not true," Henry said. "We're not speaking of Norris, Alexander. You must think. There's a new player on your board. Someone who wasn't there the other times."

I narrowed my eyes, wondering if I could squeeze a direct answer out of any of them. Brute force might be the only way.

"Who?" I said impatiently.

"Someone you've let into your home, someone who returned to us healthy and strong despite—"

"Ten years in a coma," I finished for him as the world came into sharp focus.

My God, what had I done?

.   .   .

"Do you want to discuss it?" Smith asked, showing a surprising amount of sensitivity as we took our leave.

Of course, we needed to discuss it. So, I didn't know why it was up to me whether or not to remain silent. I appreciated that he wasn't going to immediately press the issue.

My head was swimming with the suggestions, but it added up. They'd laid out the pieces for me. How had I not seen? Sarah had returned in the middle of all of this. She'd been a headache. Or rather, a distraction. But could she be the one who betrayed me? Who betrayed Clara?

Clara was kind to her. We'd opened our home to her. She was my sister.

And why after ten years would she harbour enough hatred toward me to do something so terrible?

"I can't believe and yet..."

"It makes sense," Smith said grimly. "She's been so busy acting like a fucking teenager that we didn't bother to ask some pretty obvious questions."

"I left her there," I confessed. "I knew she was there and I didn't visit. I listened to reports on her health. I...I..."

But, surely, my father had cared more. Except, he hadn't. Henry had made that clear, too. Like me, Albert had rarely visited his middle child. He'd told his brother he couldn't bear it.

And my father didn't bother pushing his comfort zone.

But it wasn't the ten years she'd lost. It was the ten years that had been stolen. Because if the Ghosts's suspicions were correct, Sarah hadn't been in a coma that whole time. What would happen to someone who was left by her family to rot and wither? How easy would it be to rend the ties that bound her to me—to her family—when no one came for her?

Now Clara was in that position, waiting and wasting away while we tried to untangle a mystery. The trouble was that every move we made only seemed to reveal a more twisted puzzle.

"What do you want to do about?" Smith asked, calling my attention back to Sarah. "Let's put Georgia on her. She can be discreet, see where she's going, and what she's up to."

"She's going to love that." I could imagine the complaints now. Georgia didn't have much appreciation for my sister and her antics. If she felt it would help Clara, she would do it though.

"Actually..." Smith trailed off, but the words he left unsaid hung between us.

"What?" I demanded.

"Georgia doesn't trust Sarah. You should speak with her."

That's what he'd been alluding to earlier when he'd questioned the pass I'd given my family. I'd thought he was insinuating Norris's guilt. Instead, he'd been attempting delicacy. Georgia had seen this. Smith had seen this. They'd known something was wrong, and I'd been too focused on my problems with my marriage and arrogantly obsessing over my feud with Anders.

"Anders." I said his name aloud, because it needed to be said.

"I thought we trusted him," Smith said carefully.

I'd thought so too, but I couldn't deny that my brother's existence had been revealed rather conveniently. Maybe it had been another tool to distract me, another carefully placed bomb, timed to go off at the right time. It hardly mattered. I needed to reassess everyone. Clara had shown me that true courage meant facing my weaknesses rather than blinding myself to them. Maybe my family was my weakness. "I don't trust anyone. Not anymore."

CHAPTER 14

CLARA

We stared at each other for a long moment as the truth trickled through me like an unwanted drug. When Rachel had mentioned what the other men called her savior, I'd gotten chills. But somehow I'd convinced myself it wasn't someone I knew.

It wasn't someone I trusted.

It wasn't someone I loved.

Because how could I ever believe anyone in my life would put me or my child in danger? How could someone in my family betray me?

I'd welcomed him into our lives, I'd fought for him, and that only made it even worse. I'd opened the door to a wolf and let him make himself at home. Never once had I suspected he was anyone other than who he said. Now my brain scrambled for clues I hadn't seen, truths I hadn't picked up on.

He'd been a bit of a loner at first, but he had good reason. Now I saw the sinister truth behind it. I'd never really met his family. I'd assumed so many things for so many reasons. Assumptions that seemed warranted then, but felt foolish now.

When he opened his mouth to speak, I held up my hand. I didn't want to hear what he had to say. It was amazing how quickly love could turn to hate.

And I hated him.

I hated him for lying.

I hated him for what he'd done to me.

And I hated him for what he would do, because I knew beyond any doubt that he would betray my best friend.

"Clara," David said, not heeding my warning, "I can explain."

"I doubt that," I spat back. Edging along the wall, I moved past him and hurried toward my room, thankful that the door locked.

But he followed, sticking the toe of his boot in the door so I couldn't close it. "Can I come in?"

He asked even as he prevented me from locking him out. What was this? Some holdover of chivalry, the remnants of our false friendship?

"I don't really have a choice, do I?" I asked. "I'm your prisoner."

He winced as though I'd slapped him. I didn't buy it. But it was an act—all of it. He'd fooled every one of us into trusting him. He'd tricked us into caring about him. I wished I could hurt him now like he'd hurt me, but a man who was willing to sell his soul like this—how could I ever injure that? Anything I did would be like a paper cut when he'd inflicted a mortal wound. My life? My family? What he'd done to us would leave a gaping hole no matter how this turned out.

"I've wanted to come and check on you," he said, taking a seat on the bed. His closeness sent nausea snaking through me.

"There's no need." We weren't family or friends or even acquaintances. We were strangers. I knew that now.

"They wanted me to wait until..." He looked away and I knew I didn't want him to finish that sentence. It could only end badly.

"Nice of you to come and visit the prisoner," I said flatly. I had a million questions for him and no desire for answers. Because I saw how this would end.

"I didn't plan this, you know," he said after a long pause. "I didn't mean to become friends with you."

"This must be so hard on you," I said dryly. "And we aren't friends. We're nothing."

"That's fair, I suppose, but I do genuinely care about you." His brown eyes were as soft and warm as ever but I couldn't trust them even though some latent subconscious affection called out to him.

"Then tell my husband where I am." Something split in my chest and tears swelled my throat. "How could you do this? To me? *To Edward?*"

"I didn't mean to fall in love with Edward," he said quietly.

"You're a monster." How could he claim to love him and do this to him? There was nothing that could ever make me hurt Alexander this way. Whatever David thought he had with his husband was a lie.

"Maybe," he admitted. "It was an assignment. I wasn't supposed to get emotionally involved."

"Stop," I said. "I don't care. I don't want to hear how you're sorry or you messed up."

"I am sorry. I did mess up." He ran his fingers over his closely cropped head. "I was in this before I knew any of you. If I could change things…"

"Don't lie."

"I'm not lying."

"You are lying," I corrected him, "but not to me. You're lying to yourself. You have a choice."

"I don't. If it was up to me…" he trailed away, his eyes skimming the walls. Someone was listening. We both knew it.

"It is up to you. It always was. You could have warned us. You could have told us the truth."

"You don't know these people. You don't know what they're capable of," he stormed, leaping to his feet and beginning to pace the room.

"I was wrong. You're worse than a monster. You're a fucking coward."

"Clara, sometimes we hurt the people we love. You know that better than—"

"Don't," I warned him a low voice. "Don't try to compare me and you. There's no comparison."

"Alexander's hurt you. He's lied to you!" He'd begun to shout as though maybe that would help get his point across.

"To protect me—to keep me safe!"

"I'm keeping Edward safe. I'm protecting him." David

turned and faced me, his face drawn with a pained mix of hope and remorse.

"You're protecting yourself," I whispered.

I knew about lies. I'd lived them. Some lies were like bad medicine, bitter to swallow but well-intended. Others were lies sold as much to the person who told them as anyone else. Most were simply self-serving—the mark of cowardice and disloyalty. I had enough experience to know what I was dealing with now.

"Get out," I muttered.

"Clara—"

We were interrupted by the arrival of my evening meal. My eyes landed on the shiny red apple propped on the side of the tray. I knew what it meant. I knew what was coming.

That's why David was here. My time was up. June had reported my latest blood pressure numbers to Dr. Rolland. I wasn't ready, but would I ever be?

"What are they going to do to the baby?" I asked him, still staring at that apple.

"Clara, the baby will be fine. No one wants to..." He broke up like he didn't want to finish that sentence.

"What?" I demanded. "I want to know. You owe me that much. Isn't that why you've come to offer a dying woman some comfort?"

The stricken look in his eyes told me that I'd hit my mark. There was no plans to let me leave here. Not breathing. He'd known that when he had come. Maybe he wanted forgiveness or absolution. Maybe they'd forced him to attend me in my final hours.

I wished they sent someone else. Anyone else.

"I wish it didn't have to be this way," he murmured.

"It doesn't," I said simply. "You chose this, so tell me what they're going to do to my child."

It wasn't solace I was seeking exactly. Looking for comfort in this situation would be like seeing relief for a headache at the barrel of a gun. There was no happy ending. Every moment had been slowly and inevitably leading to this one. My curiosity stemmed from something else entirely. They could have taken me when I was pregnant with Elizabeth. They could have seen to my death on the day of the wedding. Why now? What had changed?

"This wasn't the plan initially," he explained. "You should eat."

I rubbed my stomach. "I'm not hungry."

In truth, I was famished, so was the little prince kicking eagerly in my belly. I hoped he couldn't hear my stomach growl.

"My organization was put into place during World War II to look into the private lives of certain British citizens. After the war it was disbanded. *Officially*."

Unofficially, it seemed they were still holding staff meetings. I wondered if Alexander knew any of this.

"The world is at war again," he continued.

"No, we're not." Was that really how he justified his involvement?

"Aren't we? Nazis marching in the streets instead of hiding behind closed doors. Terrorists attacking our cities. It's only a matter of time before the next major world event," David countered, his face flashing with sudden passion. I saw the zealotry in it. That was what had driven him to these people. "Things are getting out of hand."

None of that explained why this organization had targeted my family. "What does any of this have to do with us?"

"MI-18 is a counter-measure," he explained. "We balance things out when Great Britain swings too far in one direction. When we were disbanded, the king reorganized us and set down guidelines. If the monarchy was threatened, there were contingencies in place."

"What kind of contingencies?" My stomach plummeted as I considered those contingencies were the reason I was here. It had been inevitable—a row of dominoes waiting to fall. But what had tipped the first one over?

"The monarchy has been handing control to Parliament while catering to a rapidly progressing world view for a while. As such, the crown is undermining its own power. Albert started it without even knowing," David told me, shaking his head in disgust. "When he handed over a majority of the political power over to parliament, the first contingency went into action. That contingency was supposed to ensure we had a monarch in place who was malleable to *our* plans."

"What does that mean?" I asked cradling my bump. "And what does any of this have to do with my son?"

"Initially, it was about Sarah," he said.

"She wasn't in a coma, was she?" I'd known since I met Rachel. I'd had all the pieces in front of me, I could see the big picture, but I'd refused to put them together. Still, her betrayal was nothing compared to discovering the snake in the room with me.

"No," David admitted. "With Alexander keen to tell his father to shove off, we expected he would abdicate. One push in the right direction, and we knew we could get him to do just that. When he met you, it was assumed he would abandon his title and marry you. No one thought Albert would legitimize the marriage."

"Are you claiming you're the reason I'm with Alexander?" The words tasted sour—wrong. I'd never believed in fate exactly, but the idea that I'd met Alexander because of some larger plan was ludicrous. We had found each other. We had fought for one another. It was the only truth in this world of lies.

"No, we merely encouraged things—sped them up, if you will," he said.

I recalled the stories in the papers, a new scandal coming out as soon as the last one settled. They'd brought us closer together rather than push us apart.

But no matter what he claimed, no one could have predicted that we would weather those storms. No one could feign responsibility for our love. I wouldn't allow it.

"But Alexander didn't abdicate," I said softly.

"No, he didn't," David admitted. "One of our associates found this concerning, so he took matters into his own hands. He wanted to know Alexander would be out of the picture."

"Hammond." I hated him, even more than I hated the man who'd actually wielded the gun that day. Hammond was the man responsible for Albert's death. "That plan backfired."

"Indeed. Suddenly, Alexander was on the throne, and Sarah wasn't exactly interested in playing along." David paused, glancing to the same spot he'd looked to a number of times. It must have been where the camera was hidden. But whoever was watching us hadn't intervened with his evening storytelling session. That could only mean one thing. "But then we discovered another problem. Something we hadn't counted on."

"She wouldn't go along with the plan?"

"No. It was worse than that. After Albert's death a number of private papers were stolen and we found out something we hadn't realized." David's mouth twisted into a cruel smirk. It didn't match the man I knew. Then again, nothing about this situation did. "She isn't Albert's biological child. Even if we placed her into power, she had no legitimate claim to the throne. If there was any question, the throne would pass."

"Then why were you brought in for Edward?" The timeline didn't match up. David and Edward had been an item before Albert's death, even before I'd met any of them.

"I was to become his confidant," David confessed. "I was an insurance policy in case Sarah didn't work out. Someone who saw him for who he really was, and I did a good job. Too good."

He claimed he'd fallen in love. I could see the truth of it in his eyes, but it would never erase what he'd done.

"So you wanted the throne to pass to him but I messed it up by having an unplanned pregnancy?" I was growing weary of this story, given that I'd guessed how it would end. But I still didn't have the answer as how my son played into their schemes.

"Not exactly," he said. "They planned your pregnancy. Gave you sugar pills instead of birth control."

I gasped my hands closing over my stomach.

"We knew by the time you met Alexander that Sarah would never fall into line. That made Edward our next option. But then it became clear that there was another way. Alexander would give up anything for you and that losing you..."

"Would destroy him." I searched his face for signs of remorse, there was some there hiding in his dark eyes but it wasn't enough to make me feel sorry for him. He knew what he was doing to the man I loved, the man who'd supported him and welcomed him into his family, and he was going through with it.

"I don't understand what you think is going to happen. Alexander will never cooperate with you." They had to know that. All of this so that they could convince him to abdicate?

"Alexander will lose the crown. It will be taken or it will be given up. It will then pass to Edward," David said.

"What if Sarah—" I began.

"That won't happen. Evidence would surface regarding her mental stability, and while she may not be cooperative, she knows when to heed a warning."

I wondered when they'd threatened her. Had it been under our watch? Had we been so focused on the outside that we'd forgotten to take care of our own people? The fact that David sat across from me now was my answer.

"So you'll be married to the King and you can turn his head any direction they wish," I guessed. It was a basic plan with a lot of promise. But maybe David didn't know Edward as well as I did. My best friend would catch on—wouldn't he?

"For a time," he admitted, "and then when he's ready, your son will return and claim his birthright."

"Return?" I repeated, blinking at this declaration. "From where? If his father abdicates…"

"He won't abdicate for a dead child. There's no point. Your son's legacy will remain intact."

The coldness in his voice hit me almost as hard as what he was saying.

"You're going to let Alexander believe he died. That he lost both of us," I said in broken pants. My stomach heaved but it was empty so I simply gagged and coughed on air.

I was going to be sick. That was their plan all along: to break my husband's heart—to take everything from him and watch him fade into nothing. I couldn't stop them. I didn't begin to know how.

I knew their entire plan and I had no way of helping the man I loved. I wanted to scream until I shattered like my heart was doing now. But what good would that do?

I was better than that. I had to be.

"We need to be certain he breaks," David said in a quiet voice, perhaps sensing how fragile I was. "And when your son returns with true royal blood, Edward will step aside, especially when he learns the truth."

I shook my head. "What truth?"

They would never admit what they did to Edward. David never would. He'd be by his side pretending at a marriage while carefully pulling strings whenever he could.

David paused as if he wasn't certain if he should reveal more. Then he shrugged off whatever hesitation he felt. It must be easier knowing that I was going to die. A corpse couldn't tell tales. "He isn't Albert's child either."

I stared at him as this information processed. Now, I knew enough. I didn't want to know any more. I didn't want to know any of it. Instead, I made a choice.

I looked to the tray of food, then up to the camera. They'd been waiting for this. I wouldn't make them wait any longer. Picking up the apple, I took a bite.

CHAPTER 15

ALEXANDER

Nothing was out of the ordinary. At least that was the takeaway from a five minute debriefing the next morning. By the time, Brex had finished walking through what they hadn't found, I was yawning.

"You need to sleep," Georgia chastised me.

"I need to find my wife," I snapped, rubbing my eyes. I'd resorted to coffee to keep myself awake for most of the night. But it wasn't quite enough to keep my mind sharp. No matter how much I drank.

"And when we do," Georgia said firmly, "and we will, you can't be a zombie. She's pregnant. The baby could come any time..."

"That's exactly why I don't have time to sleep." I was tired of arguing this with them. "I'm doing the best I can."

Brex and Georgia shared a look that suggested they thought my best hadn't shown up recently. It was no use calling them out on it. They were right.

I wasn't at my best, because I couldn't be without

Clara. She was my best. Without her, no matter how much I tried, I was simply half a man. How long had I wasted keeping her out of certain parts of my life? How much time had I spent denying her all of myself? And for what? To protect her? I'd failed at that.

"What about our new leads?" I asked wearily, steering the conversation away from me and my faults. After Smith's and my meeting with the Ghosts, we'd arranged a tail for both Sarah and Anders. The results were frustrating.

"Sarah is barely speaking to anyone," Georgia said, sinking into a chair with a frown. She knew she was being guided to a new topic and she wasn't happy about it. "She's ignoring Pepper's calls. She isn't leaving the house. There's been no unusual activity on her mobile."

"Maybe she's waiting for instructions," Brex said in his usual clipped and direct way. Unlike his partner, he was former military and followed unspoken commands easily.

"We don't have any proof of that," Georgia added quickly. "It's just something we should consider."

No one—not even me—was sure how I would react to proof that my sister was the one who betrayed us.

"Keep watching her," I said after a beat. "What about Anders?"

"Well..." Brex and Georgia looked at one another.

"What?" I demanded. Had I been duped twice? I'd opened my home and my heart to new family—a task I hadn't found easy. Had I been trapped by my own sentimentality?

"It's not suspicious," Brex said swiftly even as my mind spun. "But we think he caught on that he's being followed."

"Fuck," I muttered. "What gives you that idea?"

"He, uh, signaled our guy," Brex said uneasily.

"Signaled?" I frowned. "How?"

"You know." Brex made a lewd gesture at me.

"Oh." So he knew we had someone following him, and he wasn't hiding that he knew. In truth, I hadn't suspected him. Norris had run thorough checks when we'd discovered his existence. They'd been clean. I'd met his mother. If his life was a cover, even he didn't know it. But the ghosts had spooked me. I no longer felt like I could trust my gut. Because I'd never looked twice at Sarah and she'd been in the middle of this the whole time.

"What do we have on MI-18?" I asked.

"That's the bad news," Georgia said gently. "We were hoping we could scare up some interest from them."

"But they aren't taking the bait," Brex told me.

Wherever they were, they were simply burrowing deeper into their hole. They had no interest in communicating with us, which meant they had nothing we wanted or they weren't interested in sharing. Neither possibility sat well.

"What do you want us to do?" Georgia asked.

"Keep up the surveillance. Keep looking into MI-18, and..." I dropped my head in my hands, biting my tongue.

"And?" she prompted.

"If you can't find my wife, find Norris." I knew what I was asking was impossible, but with each day that passed my hope dwindled more.

I had no idea what had happened to Norris, and even though I knew that he would never leave my wife without protection, I couldn't accept that he was dead. No body. No proof.

It wasn't quite hope, but it was as close as any of us were going to get.

"We've been checking in with hospitals." Brex cleared his throat before adding, "And morgues. Nothing so far."

No body. No proof.

It wasn't quite hope, but it was as close as any of us were going to get.

"Keep looking," I ordered him. "Where's Smith?"

Georgia hesitated. "Checking on Belle. She's not feeling very good."

And she was busy taking care of my daughter. I stood, swaying a little on my feet. Brex clapped a hand on my shoulder.

"Don't take this the wrong way, Poor Boy, but you need a shower and a nap."

"What I need—"

Georgia cut me off. "What you need is to take a moment to take care of yourself. You aren't going to be able to take care of Clara like this."

"What about you?" I accused, blatantly ignoring that, while Brex needed a good shave, he was in fresh clothes—as was Georgia. I was the one who'd adopted a patina of homelessness ill-suited to my life. But how could I care about things like soap and hot water and pillows when Clara might have none of those things?

"We've been taking shifts," Georgia said. "Churchill style. A few hours of sleep while the others keep working."

"And it's your turn," Brex informed me.

"Is that an order?" I said in a low voice.

"If it needs to be," Georgia said, crossing her arms.

This was what came of choosing rebels and renegades for friends. They didn't give a shit who I was. They didn't listen to my orders. It was why I liked them. Usually.

I was halfway to my private quarters when my phone rang. It was a welcome distraction from the dread building inside me. I'd been avoiding our rooms since the morning I'd faced her disappearance. There was nothing for me there but a life I might have already lost.

I sighed when I saw the caller ID. Anders really wasn't trying to hide anything from me. "Hello?"

"Are those your guys acting like bad shadows or do I have a problem?" Anders asked.

"They're mine." I pinched the bridge of my nose. I'd told Anders some of what was going on, but that was before things had spun out of control. He had no idea why I was having him watched now. He didn't know Clara was missing. There was no point involving him.

"Is this a permanent perk?" he grumbled.

"Welcome to the family." It was easier to pretend that it was just another burden of royal life than more than that.

"Great. First, you send Miss Bossy Knickers to criticise my every move and now I have bodyguards." He paused. "What happens if I move to Australia?"

"I suggest you learn to surf." I didn't have time for this,

but it was serving to distract me from the fact that I'd arrived to my rooms.

"By the way, tell your wife to call her sister. I tried to reach her, but she's ignoring us. Is this some type of isolation torture—shove us together and see what happens if we're left to our own devices? Because I'm not sure—"

"I'll tell her," I cut him off and hung up. I didn't have time for his little problems. Once one member of Clara's family began to question her absence, others would, too. The last thing I needed was a panicked Madeline Bishop fluttering about the war room.

I paused outside the entrance to my home within Buckingham. I'd been all over the palace since the day I lost her, but I'd been avoiding this. Taking a deep breath, I pushed open the door.

It was surreal—familiar and foreign at the same time. This was my home, but the involuntary joy I usually felt when entering was absent. Instead I felt hollowed out as though I'd found myself in a vacuum. There was nothing here. All the light had gone out from this place.

Around me the little reminders of Clara sparked nothing more than a numb sadness. How long would it be before they sparked nothing at all?

I decided not to dwell on it. Instead, I went to our bedroom, hesitating near the door across the hall. Elizabeth's room. I'd been avoiding her to. Unable to face our daughter, knowing she wouldn't understand what had happened to her mother.

Knowing she might never understand.

Inside, I heard low voices though: Smith and Belle.

In a moment of self-loathing, I opened the door to find them seated closely together. Elizabeth was playing on the ground, oblivious to Belle's blanched face and doubled over position. Smith knelt beside her, rubbing her back soothingly.

Stepping in, I tried to ignore the wave of jealousy that rolled through me. It should be me coming to check on my wife. It should be Clara watching over our daughter.

It wasn't their fault that wasn't the case. They were doing what they could for me. But I resented seeing what I didn't have from some pure place inside of me that couldn't be reasoned with. As the door clicked shut behind me, Belle looked up, rearranging her slack face into a beaming smile.

"Alexander," she said, swallowing hard on the last syllable. "Come to see Elizabeth?"

My daughter who'd caught wind of her father's name flopped onto her side. Pushing onto her tiny palms, she stood and began toddling toward me, laughing and crying at the same time.

Part of me wanted to turn and bolt. I couldn't face her. I couldn't answer when she asked for "mummy." Instead I allowed instinct to take over. Dropping down, I caught her in my arms. She wrapped two chubby arms around my neck and held on for dear life as a steady stream of gibberish babbled from her.

"She misses you," Belle said without a hint of accusation. "Edward's been coming to see her, but he's been busy with the—"

She clapped a hand over her mouth, her pale face

turning visibly green. Belle was pregnant, too. Belle needed rest. I'd been too caught up in my own problems to remember that the people I considered my family had their own needs.

"I've been ordered to take a shower and a nap," I said to Smith. "I think maybe Belle could use a break. I'll take Elizabeth."

Smith mouthed his thanks as he helped a still-green Belle to her feet.

"Use one of the bedrooms if you want," I told them as I gathered a blanket and supplies.

"I'll be back soon," Belle promised, guilt clashing with queasiness on her face. She looked so pained, I could almost feel it, too.

"Don't worry about it. My place is here." I glanced down to my daughter. I wasn't ready to admit she was all I had left, but I couldn't keep ignoring that I still had her.

"Thank you," Smith said under his breath as we left the nursery.

I forced a smile, hoping I looked sincere, as we parted ways. They headed to the other end of the hall where a number of guest suites sat unused.

Now I had another problem to deal with. The truth was that although I prided myself on being a hands-on father, I had very little experience with occupying a dangerously mobile toddler while attempting other tasks.

Scouting the bathroom, I quickly shut us inside, spread the blanket of the floor, and then looked around for potential death traps. After I'd closed the door to the toilet, barricaded the linen closet and double checked for low-to-the-ground outlets, I finally stripped down to take a shower while Elizabeth occupied herself with a washcloth on the floor.

It wasn't remotely relaxing, keeping one eye on my daughter, who was busy placing the cloth on her head like a hat, and trying to scrub off the frustration that seemed to coat my every limb.

This wasn't what I'd signed up for. It wasn't how my life was supposed to be. But I was here, she was here, and I needed to do better. Clara wouldn't have avoided our child for days if I was gone. She wouldn't have let someone else play mother.

I needed to remember that I was Elizabeth's father—and that was a greater gift than some men ever knew. I was just rinsing shampoo from my hair when I opened one eye to discover the blanket abandoned. Before I could panic, I glanced down to find her face pressed against the shower stall. Smiling, I bent and placed my palm over hers. She fell back laughing. Then stood up and smashed her face against the glass again. This time I smashed my face, too.

I couldn't hear her giggles over the running water, but I felt them flooding through me. It was warmth and joy and light. It was everything that I thought I'd lost—everything I thought was missing. But it had been here all along.

Someone had taken Clara, but they hadn't taken our love. No one could do that. Elizabeth was proof of that. Nothing could ever diminish what I felt for my wife. That was why I was going to be okay—we were going to be okay. Our love existed within us. It fueled us. It drove us.

Nothing could extinguish it—and that's what made us unstoppable.

AFTER MY SHOWER, I THREW ON JEANS AND T-SHIRT. Elizabeth had begin to rub her eyes, so I changed her nappy and took her to her room. Maybe it was the tentative peace I'd made but I felt as tired as she looked.

The second I laid her into her bed, she reached for me.

"It's okay, princess. Daddy's going to be right here." I sank into the nearest armchair and grabbed a book. There was no way I'd be able to nap in my own bed anyway. I'd only read her a few lines when my own eyelids began to feel heavy.

When I glanced over, I discovered her fast asleep, curled into a ball. I'd been looking for Clara—searching for my life, my heart—so hard that I'd forgotten I had a piece of it here.

"Come to bed," Clara called to me softly.

I startled and looked over to the crib. "Maybe I should stay."

"Penny will be here," she reminded me, "and she's going to be fine."

I wasn't sure if she was talking about our new nursemaid or our daughter.

"She might wake up," I argued.

"She might," Clara agreed, "and then we'll come and get her."

I'd been against moving her into her own room at night. We'd had Elizabeth in our room since she was born. Now nearly nine months later, Clara was putting her foot down and laying some boundary lines. I'd agreed to them in theory. Now that we were actually doing it...

Clara stepped into the room, allowing her silk robe to flutter open in invitation. "Alone time. Remember, X?"

Then there was that.

We barely made it across the hall before I'd torn the robe from her shoulders. Clara met my animalistic moves with a happy sigh as I lifted her off her feet and carried her to the bed. Throwing her down, I pounced.

"Is this what you're after?" I asked, dropping a hand between her legs.

Her head fell back as she moaned, but then she opened her bright eyes and shook her head.

"No?" I stopped only to have her push me away. Before I could process the rejection and what it meant, Clara was on her hands and knees crawling to me.

"This is what I'm after," she crooned, running her palm over the thick outline of my cock.

"It's all yours, poppet." I lounged against the headboard as she unfastened my slacks and freed me. Clara's eyes stayed on me as she lowered her mouth to the crown of my cock.

I loved watching her suck me off. I loved when she would pause and run her tongue over her lips like she wanted to savour the moment.

But there was one thing I loved more. Grabbing her, I lifted her up and set her over my lap. Clara didn't resist. Instead, she circled her hips, sinking over me with delicious restraint.

Her eyes rolled back as I filled her in.

"That's it," I coaxed her, rolling myself against her. "I'll take care of you."

"Promise?" She moaned as her breath began to hitch.

"Always," I vowed. Reaching for her hip, my hand closed over silk and then she was gone. Her silk robe was in my hands but there was no Clara.

I shot out of the chair, only remembering where I was in time to stop myself from waking Elizabeth.

I didn't think. I couldn't. I'd had her in my hands. It was only a memory, but it had felt so real and it had reminded of exactly what I had to lose.

Marching down the hall, I went to Sarah's room and threw open the door. She sat up in bed, eyes rimmed with tears, expectation on her face.

"Where is she?" I demanded, tired of these games, tired of maneuvers, tired of knowing the answers might be right down the hall.

Sarah burst into tears. "I don't know."

CHAPTER 16

He was beginning to grow bored. A day had passed, at least. It felt more like two. Regardless of how they tried to screw with his senses, his internal clock regulated the hours fairly accurately. During that time, nothing had happened.

And Norris needed something to happen.

He'd managed to carefully unfasten the restraints, despite the broken bones in his hand and refasten them at the loosest setting. That meant it looked like nothing was out of the ordinary to the nurses when they came to check.

He had to wonder, though, why it hadn't occurred to anyone that his lack of escape attempts was the most suspicious thing of all. In his day, MI-18 operatives had been better trained.

He had no doubt that was who had him now. Although he hadn't worked out the why yet, he'd come up with a number of plausible scenarios. All he had from the evening of the attack was fragmented memories and they told a chilling story.

It was nearly enough to make him throw caution to the window and try his luck. But luck would only get him so far. Planning and waiting, even while the clock wound down, were much more likely to yield positive results.

He reminded himself of that every waking hour that passed without incident. He was about to release his theory when he heard shouts in the hallway and the sound of a gurney's wheels.

Norris slipped his hands through the loosened cuffs and sat up, carefully keeping his blood pressure in check until the moment he tore off the leads connecting him to the machines.

Standing, he found his legs stiff, but the more trying physical obstacle was the soreness in his lower abdomen from where he'd been stabbed. The good news was that adrenaline was already beginning to kick in. He'd collected two useful objects from the nursing staff over the last two days: a badge and a paperclip. Because he'd been bound, no one had bothered to check him for the missing items although he was certain that their disappearance had been noted.

On cue, a security officer walked into the door. Even with whatever chaos was going on outside, someone had noticed the monitors and hand delivered exactly what he needed.

"Stop," the guard ordered, reaching for his pistol.

That was his first mistake. He should have had it drawn when he came in.

A base-level security officer was no match for a man who'd been trained in six forms of martial arts. Two moves and one carefully timed chokehold and Norris knocked him out. Killing him—however much he might have liked to—wouldn't do him any good.

Within a minute, he had the man stripped and in the hospital bed. Reattaching the leads to the guard and angling the man's face carefully meant that no one would check in again until the guard failed to check in. Norris could fake that. He knew the protocols. That meant he had until a nurse went on rounds to get out of here.

The guard's uniform fit well enough. He was a little taller, but no one would notice.

Instinct took over as he made his way to the door and peeked around it. The hall was deserted. Whatever emergency had offered the needed distraction had the attention of everyone on this level.

There were two ways to escape a high-surveillance situation. The first was simple. Don't be seen before you're out. It was also nearly impossible. Given modern technology, movement could easily be tracked. Anything out of the ordinary would catch the attention of security. That meant the second way was usually the best. It also required more than an average skill level.

Blending in with his surroundings, looking like he belonged—that was the only ticket out of an MI-18 secured facility. He knew that. It's why he'd patiently waited days to gather as much information as possible before he made an attempt.

He'd only get one chance. Of course, he only needed one.

Security systems in corridors usually relied on cameras tucked in perpendicular corners at either end. Opening his door a crack meant he could see out while blocking one camera. The other quite possibly had a clear view of him. That's where the distraction came in. Whatever was occupying the entire medical staff likely had the attention of the men watching the cameras as well.

Slipping across to the nurse's station, he sank onto a stool, dropped the seat low, and swiveled it to look around at his options. The lower height of the chair combined with the higher counter would help block the cameras in the hall. There was likely one trained on the station—one that was rarely watched. No one ever worried about what was going on behind the counter.

In a regular hospital, he might be able to access the profiles of the doctors on staff, see who matched his general description, height, and build. But this wasn't county general and that sort of info wouldn't be left around. He was looking for something else. Scanning a few files, he finally spotted one with a familiar label.

Norris, James.

The paperwork inside consisted of nothing more than a few sheets of test results, mostly pertaining to blood work. Next to his own results, two more sets were printed but not labeled.

He didn't need to know more than that. It told him exactly why he was here, but not why they'd kept him alive.

They could have just as easily done the tests with him dead. Maybe someone upstairs was feeling sentimental.

Standing and determined to blend in as soon as the staff started filtering into their positions, he kept his head down as he began to move back to the corridor. But before he did, another file caught his eye. A quick scan told him that escape wasn't going to be as simple as getting out.

Not after discovering Clara was here, too.

CHAPTER 17

CLARA

Alexander swept his hands down my arms before grabbing hold of my hips. Drawing me roughly against him, I closed my eyes in anticipation. It felt like forever since he'd touched me. Now that he was here—now that his hands were on me—I couldn't remember what had kept us apart. It hadn't been important. This was what mattered.

He was what mattered.

I melted into him, allowing him to take control. He needed that as much as I needed to give in.

"Are you ready, poppet?" he asked, his eyes fixed on something behind me.

I shook my head. Not without knowing what it was. Not without knowing what I needed to do.

"Oh, poppet." His lips skimmed down my neck, sending a fluttering need directly to my core. "You have to have trust."

"I do. I trust you." Somehow I meant it but still felt uncertain. It didn't make sense.

"Not me," he said, brushing his lips over mine and earning a whimper. "Yourself. You have to trust yourself."

A leather cuff hooked over my wrist as he spoke and I looked up at him, my wide eyes reflected in his.

"But I can't do it," I argued even as my body relaxed into the restraints. I usually could when he asked me. What was different now?

"Yes, you can, poppet." He fastened the other. With one swift smile, he dropped to the floor but rather than spreading my legs, he placed his cheek against my swollen belly. "For us. For all of us."

I pulled against the restraints as the world tipped over, light blinded me overhead, and then a familiar, but unwelcome voice, filtered down to me. "Oh! You're awake."

I shook my head, trying to clear cobwebs, and make sense of where I was. My wrists were restrained but I felt the steady cold stream of an IV in my arm.

"The doctor is on the way," June said as though this might reassure me. Given that I was cuffed to a gurney, it didn't. "It's time to have the baby."

I knew that, but my heart plummeted into my stomach all the same. I'd known when David came. I'd known when the apple waited on the tray. I'd known what was coming and I knew what I had to do now.

It had been a gamble to guess that one bite might be enough to knock me out but not keep me out. All I had left was bluffing my way across the board and hoping no guessed that my erratic moves served a larger agenda.

"Is David here?" I asked her. "We didn't get to finish our talk."

We had, in fact. I'd decided that we were through speaking when I bit into the fruit. Nothing he could say would erase his sins in my eyes. I wasn't interested in hearing him beg for forgiveness as he held a gun to my head.

"I'll go find him. You relax." She brushed a hand over my head and I swallowed against the urge to vomit.

I doubted most prisoners were relaxed as they walked to the gallows. That's where I was now, waiting for death, and if I didn't play my cards right she would have me.

I tested the cuffs once she was gone but they held fast. I wouldn't be released again. I recalled my first c-section and how my arms had been tied to the table. It'd been oddly humiliating given the circumstances—a strange thing to center on when I'd spent the hours before surgery being pocked, prodded, and displayed.

Now I was spread like a sacrifice—a virgin awaiting the slaughter. But I wasn't a virgin, and I wasn't going to give in and accept this.

I was going to fight.

CHAPTER 18

ALEXANDER

We'd been over everything a dozen times and Sarah's story hadn't changed. That wouldn't stop me from forcing her to tell it again despite the caustic looks Georgia was shooting me behind her back.

"Again," I demanded.

Sarah hiccoughed before she began recounting her story. She'd been crying the entire time. "I woke up from the accident and I was told I would need physical therapy."

I nodded. That's how her story always started. I couldn't decide if that meant that she knew it cold or she was telling the truth. Norris would know. He'd also been better at interrogations.

"After a few days I asked to see my family. They told me you were gone to war and Dad was away on a goodwill tour. I believed that for a while. But then there were no calls and more time passed. They wouldn't let me go outside. They wouldn't let me call my friends. They wouldn't tell me how long I'd been out."

Either my sister had been incredibly stupid or incredibly scared—the two states were often interchangeable in my experience. I wanted to dissect all of this. Someday. Right now I was interested in the bare facts.

"Where did they keep you?" I asked.

"I don't know," she said wearily. "There were no windows. No phones. Sometimes I was taken to a hospital wing."

"And there were no windows there either?" Smith asked.

"No," she said firmly. He was testing her. He asked this question every other time she recounted the story. "Then things got weird."

"How?" Georgia hung off every word despite having listened to Sarah's story every time. She was as eager to find clues as I was. This was the first real lead we'd had.

"Describe the room you were kept in," I said.

Sarah sighed heavily and began the description again. "There was a bed, walls, a few books, a dresser with clothes —the same clothes."

"Was there anyone else there?" I asked.

"I never saw anyone. One time I thought I saw a girl but I think I was just going crazy," she admitted in a low voice.

"And you were awake the whole time?" Brex said. This seemed to be the point he was hung up on. I could understand being frustrated by the revelation, but I didn't know why he kept bringing it up.

"Yes. Mostly. I think," she added. "It was years."

Years. She'd been awake for years and none of us had

known. It didn't add up. I knew the others were doing the same calculations.

"Can you remember anything at all? Something you saw? Something someone said?" Georgia asked.

Sarah shook her head, her lower lip beginning to tremble. "I keep trying. I should have told you. I was so scared. They said they would take me back there if I told you."

I couldn't look at her. Part of me bore this responsibility. Would they have been able to pull this off if I'd visited her regularly? I might have noticed her bed at Windsmoor was empty. But I couldn't forgive her for walking back into my home and not telling me the truth. No matter what her reasons were.

Georgia was more sympathetic. "No one will take you back. You should have told us. We can protect you."

"Like you protected her?" It was an innocent question but it hit its mark.

"Our guard was down," I said tersely. "That won't happen again."

Once Clara was back behind these walls, I was never letting her out of my sight. I suspected she wouldn't argue this time.

"If there's nothing else, you should get some rest," Georgia said doing a shocking imitation of someone with a beating heart. Even Brex stared at her.

"If you need me," Sarah said. I could feel her eyes searching me, but I couldn't bear to acknowledge her. She'd told us more than we'd known for days but it wasn't enough. "I'm sorry, Alex. I didn't know they were going to take her."

I nodded. It was the most I could afford without losing my cool. She'd been stupid and selfish and scared. Traits she shared with me. So how could I blame her any more than I blamed myself?

"If you think of anything," Brex said, sounding tired.

"I'll keep trying," she promised. "But it's not going to be useful."

"I'll take you back to your room," Georgia said. She moved to place an arm round her and Sarah stiffened.

"Sorry," she murmured. "They used to say that after the tests."

"Tests?" She's failed to mention that. Then again, we'd been grilling her for location details.

"They took my blood sometimes. They told me they were checking my vitamin levels. Then they'd give me more pills or less pills." She smiled apologetically at Georgia and began to follow her out.

As soon as they were gone, we turned to stare at one another.

"I doubt those were simply blood tests," Smith said. "So what were they looking for?"

I couldn't begin to guess. It was an interesting twist but not very useful.

"Maybe we're thinking about this the wrong way," Brex said thoughtfully.

"What do you mean?" I glanced at the clock aware that I promised Belle to check on Elizabeth within the hour.

"They might have been doing something more or they might have been doing just that. Why would you check someone's blood serum levels?"

"Malnutrition," Smith mused. "Isolation therapy. Over-exposure. Lack of exposure."

As soon as he said it, Brex nodded. "Exactly. What would happen to a person who didn't go outside? Who had no windows?"

"Vitamin D depletion," Smith said. "That can cause all sorts of problems."

"But Sarah came home healthy…"

"Someone kept her that way," Brex said grimly. "Someone who would know the effects of along-term lack of sunlight."

"What are you getting at?" My brief nap hadn't done much for keeping my head on straight. Neither had the last few hours questioning my sister.

Brex walked over to the bulletin board he'd covered with photos and leads, but instead of pointing to a suspect he opened the panel I'd shown them. "These were built during the wars. Where do they lead?"

"Fall-out shelters. Other major government buildings."

"They're not just about movement. They were about protection."

"Are you saying?" I trailed away as it all began to make sense.

"They kept her underground," he said. "Now what organization would know all about fall-out shelters that were no longer used? What organization could cover that up?"

We weren't looking for MI-18 for help. We were looking for MI-18 to find my wife.

• • •

There was one other place that connected Sarah and the war: Windsmoor. Although the house sat on the outskirts of Windsor far from the nearby castle, I believed the two might be connected. It was the kind of information I should know. But finding out for certain meant digging into files.

"Don't we have secretaries who could do this?" Georgia asked as she scrolled down a computer screen.

I glanced over at her, surprised she even had to ask. "We can't trust them."

"We don't know who has contact with MI-18." Smith nodded. "We need to be extra cautious."

But if waiting around for intel was frustrating, being on the verge of the information we needed was driving me crazy. "Why don't we just go out there?"

I couldn't stand it any longer. Maybe I was too hopeful, but this was the first solid lead we'd had. If Clara was there, why were we waiting here?

"If we move on Windsmoor without proof—without knowing what we're doing—we could give them time to react," Smith reminded me.

He was right. It didn't make it any easier to wait though.

"I think I've got something." Brex strode into the room and dropped a number of blue prints on the table. The papers were yellowing with age, but they were clearly marked *Windsmoor*.

Brex spread them over the table and pointed. "This is a planned bomb shelter."

"Planned?" Georgia repeated.

"The papers are dated a few weeks before the war ended." Brex sighed, stepping back, and pausing for a moment. He seemed to know that he was either delivering good news or bad news. "If they began construction..."

They probably wouldn't have continued it after the war ended. "Why wait this long?"

England had been at war for years. It was strange to think they hadn't bothered with adding the extra protection until 1945.

"Why would they do that?" My hope flickered, the news like a dash of water to the small flame. I'd let myself believe we'd found her. "I should have known."

"Known what?" Georgia demanded, still pouring over the plans. "It could still be there. They could have finished it."

"Who?"

"MI-18," she said. "They would need a base of operations."

"I think someone would have noticed if construction continued," Smith said dryly.

Their henpecking wasn't making me feel any better.

"It's the only lead we have" I said softly.

The argument died down and the room fell silent. We all knew that the longer Clara was out there, the less likely... I couldn't even bring myself to admit what might happen.

She couldn't be gone.

"I promised her that I would protect her," I murmured. And here I was impotent and useless. I had resources at my disposal. I had a team of people willing to do whatever it would take to get her back. And still, I had nothing.

Anger ripped through me and without thinking, my hand slid over the table knocking the useless documents to the floor. A second later and the table itself flipped over. To their credit, the others didn't step in. They didn't even flinch. They let me continue wrecking the room until there was nothing left to destroy. When the last paper had been ripped off the bulletin board, I slid down into a heap as broken and ravaged as everything else here.

"So we should check it out." Brex straightened, instantly resolute.

"What's the point?" My words sounded hollow even to me, echoing from the deep emptiness inside me.

"The point is that we're not giving up." Georgia crouched down beside me, placing a hand on my shoulder. "We're going to find her, and we might as well start at Windsmoor."

I glanced up, surveying each of them as I tried to decipher if I'd pushed them to this point. "You said it yourself. If we're wrong..."

"If we're wrong, so what?" Smith said. "We need to find her and we can't wait around until we have all the information. If Norris was here, what would he tell you to do?"

I'd tried not to think too much about Norris, but I felt the same stab of pain at the mention of him. But by ignoring his absence, had I failed to consider everything he'd taught me? What would Norris do? He would know how to handle this. He would have found her already.

"He wouldn't let anything get in his way," I said. "He'd go."

Brex leaned down and scooped the blue print remnants from the ground. "Then we go."

We had no idea what we would find. Maybe we were all tired of sitting still. Maybe we all sensed the clock was winding down. Maybe we'd finally crossed the line separating rational action from bald-faced hope.

The consequences were obvious. If we were wrong, it could give MI-18 time to mobilise. But they'd plenty of time to do so already. If we were truly wrong, they were probably watching us and laughing. And if we were right, we might be walking into a trap. We might be walking in blind. I didn't care, because some love was worth dying for.

CHAPTER 19

CLARA

The door cracked open and I strained to see David peeking inside. "Clara?"

"I asked to see you," I said.

He stepped into the room, shifting uncomfortably on his heels. He didn't want to be here. That made two of us. But unlike me, he had a choice in the matter. I just needed him to see that.

"I need you to promise to look after the baby," I said.

"Clara, I…" He shook his head. "I'll do the best I can."

"You owe me," I said softly. Fiercely. "What's happening now. You did this."

"If I could change—"

"You can." I wasn't going to play into his lying game. He wasn't going to walk out of this room without facing the truth. "Let me go."

He stared at me like I'd sprung a second head. "You won't make it out of here. There's guards and security measures and…"

"Please." My voice broke on the word, desperation pouring out of me. "Please. Don't make me die like this."

"You'll die if you try to escape," he whispered, moving closer to me.

"I would rather die fighting than be gutted on some table and left as scrap." Tears rolled down my face as I considered what awaited me. When I'd taken a bite of the apple I'd known I might never wake up. There wasn't going to be a second miracle. Once they rolled me into surgery, that was when my life ended.

"The baby," David said.

"They'll save the baby." I knew that. No matter what they did to me. He would be saved. He was what they were after. He was the prize.

"You can't take that chance." But his eyes lingered over the cuffs.

"I can't lie here and wait to die," I sobbed. "Give me a chance. Help me."

"Clara." He shook his head. "I can't—"

"If you ever loved Edward—if you loved any of us—undo these restraints. You're my family. Not theirs. You promised him for better and for worse. Be better." We both knew that this wasn't going to end well. We also knew that if I walked out of here, everything would change. David wouldn't be able to hide the truth and I wouldn't lie for him. I just had to help him see that living with what he'd done would be a worse fate. "You're better than this. If you do this, it will tear him apart. You won't be able to live with yourself. Your marriage doesn't survive my death."

"And it survives your rescue?" He bit his lip, turning away from me. "You'll tell him. You'll tell all of them."

"It's never too late for redemption," I said softly.

"Do you think Alexander will believe that, too?" he said darkly. "Or even Edward? I know how he feels about lies. He thinks we don't keep them from each other."

He was spinning out of control. I was losing him, but I still needed him.

"Someone will find out and when they do, there will be no second chance for you," I said. "If you save me now…"

My final argument hung in the air between us. It was the best I had. We both knew there was no magical happily ever after waiting for all of us on the other side of this. I just had to show him that every path led to the same devastating ending—only he could contain how many hearts were broken.

"You'll never make it," he said. But he moved closer, his fingers dancing over the cuff.

"Tell me," I begged. "Anything that might be useful. I won't ask any more of you."

A muscle twitched in his jaw, but finally he spoke. "They've reduced staff for the birth. Most of the organization knows the plan, but not the details. The less people who know the details…"

The less people there were to spill them. I nodded, my breath hitching as he began to unfasten the cuff.

"If you follow the northern corridor, there's an exit to the surface." He stopped on the buckle. "Even if you get there, there's nowhere for you to go for miles."

"I'll hide," I said. It wasn't much of a plan, but I had to

take small steps. Getting out was the first bit. Once I did that I'd be able to think—once we were safe. "Which is the northern corridor?"

"Out and to the left." He exhaled sharply and then finished unfastening the cuff. I didn't wait for him to start on the second. Instead I fumbled for it. David pushed my hand away and did it himself.

Sitting up, tight pain seized my midsection and I doubled over, gasping.

"Clara," David said in alarm.

"Contraction," I panted. Why? This couldn't be happening. It was probably stress.

"They're inducing you," David confessed, moving to remove the IV from my arm.

"Inducing?" I stared at him. "Why?"

David ripped it free and shook his head. "You don't want to know."

"Why, David?" I repeated. I'd had a c-section with Elizabeth. We were waiting for the doctor now. It didn't make sense to induce me when they could easily...

"Part of the cover story," he said softly. "They planned to take you to a hospital a few hours from here, make it look like you left Alexander, and then died in childbirth."

I clapped a hand over my mouth as another contraction hit, this one stronger than the first. I wouldn't allow this to happen.

"Help me," I commanded, ignoring the tightness as I got to unsteady feet.

"Clara, you aren't going to make it," he said.

I looked him in the eyes as pain burst to fury. "I won't die like that. You don't have to help me."

Shaking off his hands, I made my way to the door. I put my hand on it as another contraction hit. My knees buckled as my mind instinctively did the math. They were coming close together—too close. Holding the door for support, I searched for some untapped strength.

But all I found was fear. I was in labor. How was I supposed to sneak out of here? My breath came quickly now, responding to the waves of contractions as well as the panic.

I wasn't going to go to sleep and never wake up. I was going to help them. I was going to bring this child into the world and see him taken from me.

David came up beside me, an oxygen mask in hand. "You should lie back down," he said soothingly, like a parent who'd just let their child fail as a lesson. "Come on."

I tried to fight him as he slipped the mask over my head and forced me back toward the bed. But the fast-coming contractions had sapped my strength. Still, I wouldn't allow it to end like this. Gathering every ounce of courage I had left, I shoved him away and stumbled one step toward the door.

As it opened, I sank to my knees only to look up and see two familiar blue eyes watching me over the barrel of a gun. Before I could process it—process him—a shot rang out.

CHAPTER 20

ALEXANDER

Brex insisted on piloting, citing my lack of sleep and general distraction as reasons why he was more qualified. I didn't bother to argue that we'd been tired and distracted on the war front, too, and that had never gotten me out of duty. It gave me time to think, even with the others talking over headsets.

"When we land, we'll head to the southwest quadrant of the estate. That's where the shelter was being built, according to the plans," Smith said. "No deviations. We need to minimise the risk of anyone spotting us."

I wanted to wish him luck trying to keep us all in line. It would be like herding cats. Then again, now we had a purpose, and even if chances were slim we would find something, there was too much riding on it not to try.

I stared out the window, watching as the sprawl of London gave way to countryside. Windsor was a short trip from Buckingham and the helicopter I'd kept on standby since taking residence at the palace had been prepped and waiting. It had still taken us nearly half an hour to depart, mostly because the others insisted on going prepared.

Something heavy landed in my lap and I glanced down to find a gun. Looking up, my eyes sought Smith's. We'd discussed this. I knew it would come to this. But now that we were here—on the verge of finding her—I knew I wouldn't hesitate to kill anyone who came between me and her.

I'd once thought my father sent me to war as punishment. Now I wondered if he'd known a war was coming my way all along.

I was prepared. I'd seen death. I'd killed.

And I would do it again.

Windsmoor was eerily quiet as we landed the helicopter on the grounds. There had always been something strange about the house, and now it stood empty and lonely, making it even stranger. After Sarah had woken up, the employees had been dismissed or reassigned. I'd been avoiding the question of what to do with the estate ever since. Turning it into a summer house was out of the question, as was gifting it to a family member. It felt wrong—perverse somehow—to do anything with it at all. It had been a house of secrets. It was the place where we stashed the past we didn't want to confront.

Now, being drawn back here, I realized it had become something else entirely. Knowing Sarah's story, knowing that my family's lie had provided cover for a much bigger lie, made the place feel more sinister. It was a warm spring day, but the closer we got to the house the colder I felt.

I was more than happy to let Smith take the lead on this one. I had my own ghosts to battle here.

"According to the blueprints, the entrance will be exterior." Smith pointed to a patch of nondescript lawn. "Somewhere around here."

As we moved toward the area, I felt morale tank. The lawn was untouched. If this was where the bunker was placed, it didn't look like anyone had used it in years. It might not be here at all.

"I'll grab supplies," Brex called, hiking a finger towards a potting shed.

We were all eager for answers and knew we had to dig for them. I pushed aside the doubt creeping through me and forced myself to move forward. When Brex handed me a shovel, I got to work. It only took a few minutes before Georgia shouted. "Here!"

She'd hit upon a metal door, long forgotten under grass and dirt. Dropping my shovel, I ran to her and heaved it open. It was dark inside, but I didn't care. I didn't wait. I went down the ladder before anyone even had a chance to shine a flashlight.

As I descended, I felt my mood descend as well. Just because there wasn't a hint of life didn't mean Clara wasn't here. I hit the ground with a crunch, landing on an unfinished dirt floor. A moment later, Brex joined me, shining a flashlight into the empty space around us.

The bomb shelter looked like it had only gotten to the foundational stages. A few retaining walls were done, but another had been left unfinished. It had begun to crumble after years of disuse.

"This would have led into living quarters." Brex took a few steps toward a doorway, but paused. "They didn't even bother."

We'd known what we were going to find when we saw the dates on those plans. There was no reason to continue building a fall-out shelter after the war drew to a close. Not even the most judicious minds wanted to linger on wartime sorrows. After the bombs fell, everyone believed no war like that would ever be fought again. They were right.

Now, war was more protracted and more cruel. Now, war found its way into the streets of cities for deadly one night stands. Now, war knocked on your door and took you to battle one-on-one.

I knew because war had found its way to me.

"We should go back up," Brex coaxed. "Regroup."

Regroup? What was the point? We were as clueless as when we'd first began. I was vaguely aware of climbing the ladder, my body propelling me up the rungs while my mind stayed below.

I'd been holding on to Clara's light the last few days, but I couldn't see it anymore. Not a flicker. Not a flame.

Part of me wanted to tell them to close the door and leave me here to rot. I didn't deserve more than that, and when sunlight hit my face, I wanted to throw myself back down the hole.

Georgia studied me, her dark eyes inscrutable. I could only imagine what she saw: weakness, failure. But she didn't comment on that. "Let's go inside."

The last time I'd entered this house, I'd been full of dread. Clara had found out my secret. I'd thought then I might lose her. I'd deserved to. Now I wish I had. If she'd left me, none of this would have happened. She would have been safe. But I had been selfish.

In the few months since Windsmoor had been vacated, it had begun to collect dust and cobwebs. Although security checked in on the house, I'd assigned no temporary or permanent staff to keep the grounds or interior orderly. I'd wanted to put this place and what had happened here behind us all.

But Windsmoor didn't want to let us go.

I bypassed Smith and the others, who'd spread the house's blue prints on the table looking for some other lead, and headed down the narrow hall to the room where Sarah had slept all those years.

Except Sarah hadn't been there. If I'd visited I might have known that. Where had they kept her? Who had kept her? Why? Each door I passed seemed to ask another unanswerable question.

When I opened the door to her room, it was as empty as the unfinished bomb shelter. The hospital bed was gone, as were the machines. There was no nurse sitting bedside. It was simply an ordinary room that held no memory of what it had once been.

"I'm sorry." My words echoed in the empty chamber. I didn't know who I was speaking to—I didn't know who I'd wronged—but I needed to say it. "I wish I could undo it all. I wish I could erase all the pain I've caused. I wish I could pay for my own sins."

Because Clara was paying for them while trying to protect our unborn child. She'd paid my debts over and over. Because Norris had given his life for my family. He'd given everything for me. Loving me wasn't worth the price.

"This isn't your fault," Georgia's voice punctured the silence.

I couldn't bring myself to face her. She knew better than most what I was capable of—the monster lurking behind the man.

"Isn't it?" I asked. "I knew better than to fall in love with her. I knew this life would destroy her."

"You knew about this?" Georgia snorted and moved beside me.

"I knew my family was fucked up," I said.

"Every family is fucked up. You didn't choose this life."

"But I chose her." It was the same inexorable truth I kept coming back to. I'd chosen her against reason and common sense and public opinion.

"You chose happiness," Georgia said softly, "which is what we all want—and that wasn't stupid or selfish. It was brave. It takes guts to choose to be happy. Most people aren't strong enough to do it. I'm not."

"Why?" I didn't understand, because I no longer felt brave or happy.

"Because being miserable is easier. It's humanity's natural position. We invent technology to make our lives simpler but not happier. We pretend everything is okay when it's not. We fake happiness because the real thing has to be worked for. You fought for Clara. She fought for you."

"I'm tired of fighting," I admitted to her.

"I know." She placed a hand on my back. "But choosing

happiness is the best revenge. Refusing to suffer when others want you to eats away at them."

"If you know this, why aren't you happy?" I leveled a gaze at her. We'd danced around this since she'd come back into my life. For all of Georgia's confidence and courage, she hadn't been happy for a moment. I don't think I'd ever seen her happy once.

"That's not how my story goes." Her eyes were haunted as she spoke. "I only know happiness because I've seen it. I've never...felt it. The closest I've ever come. Well, you know."

I'd seen Georgia's files. I knew things about her past, she would never speak of, so I understood that she'd been broken. But it filled me with pity to know that she equated happiness with nothing. That oblivion was as close to bliss as she'd ever come.

"I hope that's not true someday," I murmured.

"Me too."

"There you are!" Brex called from the doorway. "Look, I don't know, but I think we found something."

It took effort to turn and follow him. It was another dead end. I knew it. When we reached Smith, he held up the blue prints.

"This house doesn't make sense," he said.

I shrugged. I'd always felt that way about it. "These old estates never do."

"Not the actual house," he clarified. "The blue prints clearly show the exterior square footage, but when you come inside—"

"It's too small," Brex said. "We just went through the

whole house. It doesn't add up."

"Either the walls are really thick or…"

"There's something behind them," I finished for them. It made sense. Windsmoor was adjacent to Windsor Castle, which, like Buckingham, utilised a number of hidden passageways to help royalty move about while the guests used the stairs and halls.

"What's interesting is that it's not in the blue prints," Smith said.

"But they wouldn't have added them later." It didn't make sense. "Why wouldn't they have included the passages on the blue prints, especially if the aim of the plans was to make Windsmoor more secure? The passages could have linked to the bomb shelter."

"Because they didn't need to make it more secure," Brex said. "Think about it. Why draw up plans a few months before the war ended? They knew it was drawing to a close."

"And why leave out the passages?" Smith added.

"Because you didn't want people to know the truth. You wanted to send them in the wrong direction." It was starting to become clear. The fallout shelter was a diversion, meant to keep people from looking closer at Windsmoor.

"There's a shelter here somewhere," Smith said. "I'm sure of it. They've left it off here on purpose."

No one asked why. That reason was clear. Someone didn't want it to be found.

"Where do we look?" I asked.

The high-pitched siren of an alarm answered me.

CHAPTER 21

CLARA

Pain doubled me over as a strong arm wrapped protectively around me. I couldn't bring myself to look up. "Clara, we need to move. They'll have heard that."

As if on cue, a siren blared outside the door. We were out of time, but now I wasn't alone. Now I had someone by my side who would get me out of here. I struggled to my feet with Norris's help. As soon as I was up, I threw my arms around him and began to cry.

For the first time in days, I felt safe. Warmth swirled around me like a blanket as Norris wrapped me tightly in a hug.

"It's okay, Your Majesty. I'm here."

I twisted my head, bracing myself before seeing what had happened only moments ago, but Norris tried to shield my view.

"No, don't turn your head." He tried to keep me from looking back to where David had stood, but I turned anyway.

I wasn't certain what I'd feel. I hated him. I loved him. But the sight of David strewn across the floor, hands clutching a bloody wound made me sway on my feet. Norris kept me upright.

"Clara," David called weakly, stretching out a hand. "Please..."

Part of me wanted to go to him. Part of me hated the idea of him dying alone. He was my brother—or he had been. We'd commiserated over falling in love with royal men. I'd picked out his wedding band. We were supposed to be family.

The rest of me remembered how he'd tried to haul me back to the bed. He was going to let them kill me. He was going to choose cowardice over family. Why shouldn't I do the same?

"We only have a moment," Norris warned me. "We need to get a move on. Someone knows I'm free."

"It's...an...evacuation," David said, shaking his head. "The siren only goes off when a location has been burned."

Burned? That meant nothing to me, but Norris's eyes narrowed. "Then we have even less time if protocol is the same."

"Five minutes." David waved his outstretched hand and for the first time I realized he was holding something in his bloody palm: his security badge. "This will get you out. Take the northern corridor."

"What about the my room? Rachel?" I asked. She was there. She was trapped. Or would they take her with them?

"There's an exit on the east end of the cell block, but you don't want to go down there. There are..." He coughed and a small fountain of blood trickled down his lip "...explosives. Counter measures."

Norris covered me as we approached David, keeping the gun trained on him the whole time. He whipped the badge from his hand and backed me away.

David's head lolled a little as he tried to reach for me. "Tell Edward I love him. I'm sorry. You need to go. Don't bother with..."

The words faded from his lips as his head tipped to one side.

"Is he..." I couldn't bring myself to ask.

"He will be," Norris said grimly. He glanced at the flimsy hospital gown I had on just as another contraction hit.

I bent forward, crying out. It felt like I was being torn in two. My hands instinctively covered my womb. The baby couldn't come now. Not like this.

Norris kept a hand on the small of my back, looking ill at ease about our situation. The man could walk into a room shooting, yet it only took childbirth to make him uncomfortable. "I'm sorry, but we have to go. If this building has been burned..."

He didn't have to finish the sentence. Smoke began seeping under the door frame. Norris let go of me and wrenched a sheet off the bed. Tearing a swath he held it to my face. I took it, grateful.

"You ready?" he asked.

The corridor outside was chaos, but no one seemed to notice or care that we were there. Then again, Norris was wearing a guard's uniform. He kept the gun out, but no one stopped us. The few personnel we came across seemed occupied with their own tasks. A few had files. Others were racing up the northern corridor. When Norris turned to lead us that way, I shook my head.

"This way." I pointed back to the corridor that led to where they'd kept me and Rachel.

"We need to leave."

I pulled out of his grasp, prayed another contraction was a long way off, and started toward the other end. Rachel's life had been stolen from her. She'd been an unwitting pawn in this bizarre game and I wasn't about to sacrifice her now.

She had answers whether she knew it or not. And she deserved better than being left to die.

Norris came up beside me, shaking his head. "It's dangerous."

"I know, but I have you now." I would not have dared to go back for her until he showed up.

When we reached the door that led back to the rooms I'd been kept in, Norris scanned David's badge. It clicked open.

The smoke was thicker in the corridor and I coughed, crouching as low as I could, where the air was clearer. I pointed to the end of the hall, where Rachel's room was. It would be the farthest from the eastern exit, if I had my bearings. Norris held up a hand as if wanting me to wait here. I watched as he raced down the hall. A moment passed. When he didn't reappear, I hobbled down the hall, trying to ignore the first pangs of the next contraction. When I got to her room, I found him hunched over the bed. Moving inside, I realized he was performing CPR.

But there was no use. Rachel's eyes were turned up to the ceiling, her hand splayed across the bed, and on the floor lay an apple.

When Norris turned and shook his head, I already knew. This time they'd put something deadly in her food. I choked back an angry sob as the contraction robbed me of my grief.

Norris didn't wait for it to pass. Instead, he lifted me in his arms, abandoning the gun and started down the hall. I turned my face into his shoulder, trying to block out the smoke. His heart was beating fast and I could hear his lungs struggling to keep up with the polluted air.

He stopped at the door we'd come through, but there was no scanner here. It could only be opened manually. That meant we had to find the exit David had told us about.

"I can walk," I told him, squirming in his arms. It would be faster, barring any more contractions.

Once we reached the far end of the hall. We began opening doors. Then I remembered where I'd woken up. Opening that door, we walked into an empty room. I'd looked for windows that day, but I'd never bothered to look up.

Norris had the same thought. He pointed to the ceiling where a thin line formed a barely visible circle. This was the eastern exit? No wonder David had warned us the other way.

Norris disappeared into the hall and came back

carrying a chair from Rachel's room. He stood on it and reached for the circle, pushing against it. But before he got it to budge, a cold voice sliced through the air.

"I wouldn't do that."

I whipped around to find myself staring at a ghost.

Norris stopped and slowly got off the chair, looking unsurprised to find himself in the same room as Jack Hammond.

"You're dead," I said, still staring at him.

"Only as dead as you, my dear." He brandished a pistol in our direction. "Which is to say *very* if you keep trying to force your way out this exit. It's wired to explode."

"Hammond." Norris nodded. "If you know that, you know the way out."

"You mistake why I'm here. Like your darling queen, you assumed this section was empty, but some of the doors were locked."

"But then..." He had been here the whole time? I shivered, remembering how I'd found myself here, naked and alone. But I hadn't been alone. The man who had conspired to kill Alexander's father had been here the whole time. "But June said there were no more prisoners."

"Prison means different things to different people, especially June." Hammond motioned for us to move away from the chair. "For some people, it might mean being stuck overseeing a nearly empty prison block because you pissed off the higher ups. I've wasted years here, doing nothing, waiting for a second chance to prove myself. But I was stuck after your husband tried to kill me."

My mouth fell open. Almost immediately I began to cough as too much smoke got past the cloth barrier.

"Careful now," Hammond drawled, "don't get worked up and have that baby on the floor. You're surprised to hear your husband killed a man? Well, tried to kill a man."

I looked to Norris and realized his eyes were still hard. This news hadn't surprised him, which meant it was true.

"That's the thing about our little organization, isn't it, Mr. Norris? They can save just about anyone when they want to."

"I don't understand." I took a few steps away from both of them. "Your organization?"

"My former organization," Norris said quickly. "I haven't been with MI-18 in decades and Hammond knows it."

"You're never really out. I thought we sent you that message quite clearly a few years ago." Hammond shrugged. "I guess you didn't understand."

"No, I've simply never chosen to allow anyone else to determine my fate." Norris didn't try to move closer to me, but he stepped between us just as another contraction hit.

"Now, Norris, she doesn't look good. You're sealed in here and she's about to have a baby."

"Get to the point, Jack," Norris demanded.

"I can help you out of here, but you must do two things."

"If you think I'm going to help you, you piece of—"

"Now. Now. I'm the one with the gun and the one who knows that, in less than a minute, every explosive in this corridor will detonate to ensure scorched earth. You remember what that means, right?" He pointed the gun over his shoulder at me. "She won't make it out of here without my help."

"What do you want?" Norris spit out.

"They're very simple requests. You should have no issue fulfilling them," Hammond said with a smirk.

We were running out of time, if what he said was true, and he was acting like this was all a game.

"First when we get to the ground, you're going to let me go."

"MI-18 won't let you stay loose for long," Norris said in a low voice.

"That might be true, but I'll take my chances. Something tells me Alexander will be more specific in his shots this time and I have my own affairs to wrap up."

Norris eye's darted to me, and I nodded. We had to think of the baby and Hammond was our best shot out of here.

"And the second thing?" Norris asked. I didn't understand how he could stay so calm. Between the gun, the sirens, and the smoke, I felt like I was having a panic attack. It definitely wasn't ideal labor conditions.

"I want you to tell me the truth. I want to hear you say it," Hammond sneered as though this was his real prize.

What truth? I waited for Norris to respond, but he stood silently. "You already know. I don't need to confirm it. I've seen the files."

"But I want to hear it from your mouth. I want to hear you say how you betrayed the royal family." Hammond lowered the gun. This was a confession he wouldn't take by force, but I didn't understand what he meant.

"I betrayed no one." Norris hadn't changed position. He'd shown no sign of guilt.

"Then no deal. We all die here." Hammond lifted the gun once more. "Would you like me to make it quick? I'm sure she would. She's already in enough pain."

Norris's eyes flashed to me, crinkling around the edges as he regarded me. Something unrecognizable passed over his face before he closed his eyes.

"Please," I begged him. "I can't do this much longer."

My lungs were beginning to burn from smoke and the contractions were coming more closely together. I cried out as another one hit, and then Norris confessed to the last sin I'd ever expected him to commit.

CHAPTER 22

ALEXANDER

Where there's smoke, there's fire. The alarms ringing through the house didn't seem to have a source. That didn't stop them setting off the sprinkler system. Water sprayed overhead and we dodged left and right, trying to evade it as much as possible. Our tactical gear kept it from soaking into our clothes, but slippery weapons didn't help anyone.

"There!" Someone yelled, the alarms nearly drowning him out.

Tendrils of smoke were seeping out of crack in the paneling. The fire was in the house. We just couldn't see it. That meant we'd been right about the passageways. It couldn't be coincidence that somewhere deep inside this hell house someone had lit a fire.

They were here, and now they knew we were here.

"If it's like the ones at home." I studied the wall looking for a likely trigger point and found a button hidden neatly in a painting's frame. When I pressed it, a panel slid open. Smoke billowed out, but none of hesitated.

"Should we mask up?" Brex asked, gesturing toward the protective shield dangling from his helmet.

"We need to be able to communicate." We'd thrown together our gear at the last minute, which meant we didn't have a comms system to fall back on. "If it gets bad..."

They could use their judgment. For now, we needed to be able to get each other's attentions, especially with the noise spilling through the open panel. It would be worse once we reached the bunker hidden under the house.

"Weapons out," Smith shouted.

Now that we were closer to the source of the chaos, it was even harder to get bearings. The alarms inside Windsmoor sounded like wind chimes compared to the screeching fall-out bells running on continuous loop down here. We followed them, knowing we were heading in the right direction as they got louder.

None of us knew what waited for us on the other side. Then again, it didn't really matter. We'd all come here for one purpose. It united us now.

But it didn't prepare us.

The door we found at the end of hidden hall might have been impenetrable if someone hadn't left it ajar. Pushing it open, we stepped into the remnants of a hospital wing. Bright white walls, exam rooms, flickering fluorescent lights—it might have been any hospital except for its current state. It looked as though it had been abandoned in a hurry, papers and files strewn everywhere, a gurney knocked on its side. But there wasn't a living soul around.

"Alexander!" Smith called and I turned to find him staring, white faced into a room. I couldn't imagine what had shaken a man like him. Moving to it, I pulled back the curtain and nearly collapsed.

In the center was a hospital bed surrounding by monitors. A blue curtain was hung across its center and a cart of surgical implements waiting next to it. It might have been used for anything but on a stainless steel table next to a small scale sat a baby blanket.

"It hasn't been used," he said, coming up next to me.

But it was here. She was here. I didn't know if that made me feel better or worse.

"Find her," I called out. We'd taken a few steps when a small explosion burst through a wall down the hall. Plaster ricocheted toward us and we ducked for cover. I threw myself behind a nurse's station, barely missing a stool. When the initial shock was over, I pushed myself up, steadying myself with the desk counter.

"Is everyone okay?" Georgia yelled, shaking bits of plaster from her hair.

I heard a few more shouts but didn't answer her. I was distracted by a file laying on the counter.

Norris, James.

Throwing it open, I tried to make sense of the reports, but it was full of cryptic test results. The one thing I could make out was the date. These tests had been performed earlier this week. I pulled the sheets out, rolled them up and shoved them in my pocket.

"What's that?" Smith asked, tipping his head to the papers.

"Not sure, but I think we might have found more than we bargained for." I flashed him the file folder, and his eyes widened.

We'd given up Norris for dead. Maybe he was. Maybe his captors had executed him after these tests. But he had been here a few days ago—alive.

I had found him and I knew that meant I'd found Clara, too. But my brief joy was eclipsed by another explosion.

"They're bringing this whole place down," Brex said, grabbing my arm. "We need to get back to the surface."

"Not without them." I shrugged out of his grasp.

"You can't go in there, Poor Boy. I won't allow it." He stepped into my path.

"You're going to stop me?" I wasn't walking out of here without Clara.

"Not this shit again." Brex groaned and I could have sworn his trigger finger twitched a little. "We'll look. I can't let you go."

"We'll go in," Smith said, stepping beside him. Together the two formed a formidable wall, but that wasn't going to stop me from going through them.

"Like hell you will." Georgia stomped over to Smith and got in his face. "You're going to be a father."

"So is he," Smith bit out.

"If Belle was in here, you wouldn't listen to any of us." She was right and we all knew it.

"Look, for all we know, they've taken her topside," Brex argued as I pushed past him.

He had a point. She was too valuable to leave behind, but without knowing what triggered the evacuation, I couldn't be certain that she was safe. "I can't risk it. I have to know."

This time Georgia took the lead, pointing down the corridor we'd come in through. "You two get up there and make certain that they aren't taking her away right now. We'll make certain the building is clear."

Brex glowered for a moment before he finally nodded and jerked his head toward the exit. A moment later, their two hulking forms had faded into the smoke and ash swirling through the false hospital.

I charged after Georgia who'd continued down the hall, checking rooms as she went. But Clara wasn't here. Somehow I could feel her though. It was as if her presence grew stronger with each step I took. She was near. Or she had been. The truth of it vibrated in my bones. My body was on edge, longing for her nearness. She was close-by, and soon she would be back in my arms.

And I would never let her go again.

The closer we came to her, the more my body hummed with certainty. When we reached a nondescript door at the end of the corridor, I didn't think twice about pushing it open.

Georgia wedged it with a piece of debris, pointing to a wire that was peeking through the frame. It was either wired to explode or wired into a security system. I nodded, grateful she'd caught it.

The open door also helped cast light into the dark passage we found beyond the door. Smoke had built inside the space, which had to be far from the main house and deeper underground, because it had nowhere to go.

She pointed to the masks we'd kept off during the initial breach and we both tugged them over our mouths. It would make communication impossible, but it would help to filter some of this shit out. Continuing down the hall, we discovered a number of rooms, each with a bed and a dresser and little else. Was this where they'd kept Sarah?

Georgia's eyes met mine through the mask and I knew she was thinking the same thing. It matched up with the description Sarah had given of where she'd spent the majority of the last ten years. The prison was strange. It was more like a bad hotel with no windows but locks on the doors. This is what my sister had been banished to for her entire adult life. I'd left her here to rot because I'd been too cowardly to face what I'd done. I wouldn't make the same mistake again.

When we encountered a locked door, Georgia started to move past, but I had to be certain it was clear. I couldn't risk leaving Clara here. Aiming my pistol at the lock, I blew it open.

Clara wasn't inside, but it was like looking into my nightmare. A crib sat in one corner, a teetering mobile dangled bears over the mattress. There was a small changing table in the corner stacked with nappies and layette. There was no rocking chair. There were no windows.

And that's when I knew exactly what MI-18 had been after all along.

They wanted my child.

Georgia grabbed my arm and pulled me back from the door. I stumbled after her, my stomach churning. When we reached the final room. Inside a form lay on the burning bed. Thick, black smoke made it impossible to see inside. It was too slight to be Clara, but we couldn't just leave them there.

Running in, I bent down to check the woman's pulse, but froze as I got a closer look at her. Dark hair sprawled around her waxen face—a face that looked a little too much like someone I knew. But it wasn't Sarah. My mind was only playing tricks on me. Or maybe MI-18 were the ones playing tricks.

Georgia took over, grabbing the woman's wrist before looking up to me with a grim shake of the head.

Whoever she was—whatever she was here for—she was gone. They'd left her to die. How could I be sure they wouldn't do the same to my wife?

When we hit the hall, I barreled toward the rooms at the other end, but Georgia grabbed my sleeve. Ripping off her mask, she shouted, "We have to go."

I shook my head. There was no way I was leaving until I was sure.

"She's not here." Georgia began to cough without the benefit of the ventilation. "She's gone."

I paused long enough to feel the truth of this. She'd been here, but Clara wasn't here any longer. There was no light in this place. I felt foolish for falling deeper down the rabbit hole. Now I could only pray that Smith and Brex had gotten topside in time.

Making our way back through the deserted hospital

wing toward the entrance to Windsmoor, we were stopped by a shadow. A figure lurched out from a room, clutching a wound in his stomach. We kept our guns trained on him until he came into better view.

I lowered my weapon automatically. Georgia kept hers up.

"Alexander." I couldn't hear David's wheeze over the fall-out alarms but I saw my name form on his lips. Pain was written all over his face as he tried to staunch the wound in his abdomen.

I should move to help him, but I couldn't process what he was doing here. Had he followed us for some reason? Why would he risk his life when he wasn't trained in this type of situation? Then another, horrifying thought occurred to me. Was Edward here? I looked around, worried I might find my brother nearby.

David seemed to sense why I was panicked and shook his head. But the reassurance was short-lived when he mouthed something else, "She's gone. I'm sorry."

It took a moment for these words to register. Maybe I didn't want to hear them for what they were, but I couldn't ignore what he was really saying.

It was an admission. It was a revelation.

It was a confession.

I didn't think about what came next. I didn't ask any more questions. I was the law of this land, of this place, of this family, and he was guilty.

I shot him without a second thought.

CHAPTER 23

CLARA

There wasn't time to process his confession, so when Norris wrapped a steadying arm around me and helped me follow Hammond, I went with it. Besides, I had other things on my mind—like contractions that were coming approximately two minutes apart. I'd barely began to catch my breath from one when another started.

All I could think of was getting out of here, putting one foot in front of the other, and escape. We were so close. No guards barred our exit. Even the alarms had begun to fade or maybe I was just growing use to them. The eastern exit wasn't in the room I'd led Norris to, but rather concealed behind a panel in the hall.

Hammond opened it and gestured to me. "Ladies first."

I stared up at the ladder, wondering how on earth I was going to make it up or open the hatch above.

"C-c-can't," I panted, my breath catching.

"Let me." Norris moved in front of me.

Hammond didn't comment. He seemed at ease with

whatever situation left him holding a gun to our heads. And Norris couldn't act while I was stuck below with our enemy.

He shimmied up the ladder quickly. A second later and a hard twist of metal, a circular ray of sunlight broke over my head. Tears filled my eyes as its warmth washed over me.

I hadn't hoped I would ever see the sun again. Now it was so close that I could feel it. But before I could make my way up, Hammond shoved me to the side. "I think it's safer if Norris has to wait for you."

Safer for him, I was sure. I clung to a metal rung, riding out my labor pains as Hammond ascended and disappeared to the top. Overhead, I heard shouting. Then a shot. I took a deep breath and forced myself up two rungs. It was harder than I'd feared. Between my swollen stomach and the exhaustion already starting to take over my body, I wasn't sure I could make it.

"Clara!" Norris's face appeared overhead.

"I'm trying," I cried, tightening my grip as I breathed through a contraction. I was going to have this baby on a ladder if I didn't find the strength to keep going.

I thought of my son. I thought of how much he needed me to get to the hospital. And I thought of his father.

Alexander was up there. Alexander was waiting for me. I would hold Elizabeth soon. The life I'd begun to say farewell to was now back within my grasp.

My love for them was all it took. Gritting my teeth, I continued upward until Norris's hand grabbed hold of my arm, lending his strength to my climb. When my head finally emerged into the sunny afternoon, I nearly fainted.

Norris helped me up and out, and I looked around to get an idea of where we were. The grounds were oddly familiar, but before I could figure out where I was, I spotted Hammond. He had the gun raised and leveled at us.

"I'll be going now," he called. "But I'm sure we'll see each other again, Your Majesty."

"You'll die before that happens," Norris promised.

"I wonder how she'll feel—how they'll all feel—when the truth comes out. I believe you'll find aid closer to the main house." He tipped his head, the closest to a sign of deference I was likely to get, and bolted toward a hamlet of trees.

"Are you okay?" I asked Norris, looking for a signs of a wound. That's when I noticed a dark, wet spot on his shirt.

He shook his head. "He didn't get me. My wound's reopened."

The one he'd gotten on the night they had taken us. But that had been a lifetime ago—or maybe only days. I no longer knew what had happened. My own time was now measured in labor pains.

"We need to move closer to the house," Norris urged me, concern washing over his face. He was a smart man. He knew we didn't have long before I'd be past the point of no return and having this baby in some field was not an option.

"What house?" I asked, gripping the arm he offered for support. Grass crinkled beneath my feet, soft and lush. It felt like heaven. I loved everything about this world, especially being back in it.

"Windsmoor," he said, looking ahead.

That made sense. They'd kept Sarah nearby. Rachel could easily have been switched out as needed for curious doctors. I wondered how much someone like June had known. I wondered how much any of them.

Or cared.

I followed his gaze to where the once grand house sat ablaze on the edge of the grounds. I was glad to watch it burn, the fire taking the lies and deceit with it.

I didn't want to go near it, however. Some darkness still lingered around it and it felt as though it might swallow me back up. I never wanted to return to that yawning abyss—to the darkness and despair that permeated its walls.

We'd made it a few paces closer when two soldiers came racing toward us. My heart stopped and I nearly crumbled to the ground. We were so close. Norris shoved me behind him. But we were unarmed and up against two men in tactical gear holding pistols.

"She needs medical attention," he shouted. I knew Norris wouldn't let them hurt me, but what if they hurt him? We couldn't have come this far only to fail now.

The next two things happened so quickly that I wasn't sure any of it was real. Maybe I was still asleep, that bit of apple keeping me in this insane dream.

I felt a gush of warm water stream down my leg and one of the guards dropped his gun. I'd just began to process that my waters had broken when the man whipped off his ventilation mask.

Smith.

And if that was Smith, then...

I collapsed against Norris with relief as the second man holstered his weapon and did the same.

Brex.

My heart plummeted. I was safe, but it wasn't the man I'd hoped to find behind that mask.

"We've got a helicopter." Brex hitched a thumb over his shoulder.

Norris moved to lift me into his arms, but Smith shook his head.

"We've got this. Here." He bent down and picked up the gun he'd dropped. Handing it to Norris, he said, "We don't know what's out here yet. Cover me."

Norris took the weapon as Smith lifted me into his arms and began jogging toward the helicopter.

I was leaving. I was safe.

"Alexander?" I asked, scared for the first time of what his answer might be.

Smith kept his eyes head. "He's still inside. He had to be certain you were out."

Still inside? I recalled the bombs and Hammond's warnings.

"He needs to get out," I shrieked, trying to pull away from him. "You have to warn him."

"He'll get out," Smith said firmly, not allowing me to squirm away. "But he will never forgive me if I let you take another step toward that house."

"But—"

"The baby's coming, Clara." That put an end to the debate. Even I couldn't argue.

And the baby needed to be at a hospital. I didn't put up

a fight as he helped me into the back of the helicopter.

"Do you want to lay down?" he asked. I shook my head. Norris got in beside me and Brex must have reached us because the blades overhead began to turn.

"What about Alexander?" I yelled.

"He'd want you to come first. We'll come back for them," Smith promised.

Alexander would come. He would make it out of there. I tried not to think of the smoke or the flames.

He would be find and we would find each other. It was just that...

I'd expected him to be here. To walk in and carry me off like we were in a fairytale. That's how love stories ended. But even as disappointment cracked through me, I knew that our story wasn't ending. It never would. I would find him. He would find me. We always found each other.

Someone tried to place an oxygen mask over my face but I pushed it away. I could handle this with or without him. His strength was with me even if he wasn't. That's what love meant. Love filled in the parts of you that you never knew were missing. He was here with me now and then...

There he was.

Alexander.

Our eyes met across the space, and then there was no chaos, no yelling, no fear. My heart stopped and restarted in rhythm with his. Maybe it hadn't been beating this whole time.

He looked worse for the wear as though he hadn't been sleeping either. Dark stubble shadowed his jawline and his hair, which was usually combed into submission these days, was an unruly black mess. I wanted to tangle my fingers through it and pull him against me.

Yesterday, I'd thought I lost him forever.

This morning, I struggled to remember the taste of his kiss.

An hour ago I wasn't certain if he would ever hold me again.

But Alexander always found me, even the times I hadn't wanted him to. I'd clung to his memories while we were apart, building him until he felt almost real. But he'd been nothing but an illusion then. This man? He was flesh and blood and anger and love. He was real, and he was mine.

And seeing him was like coming home.

CHAPTER 24

ALEXANDER

Clara. She was here. She was real.

I tugged off my tactical gear and tossed it to Georgia as I ran towards the helicopter.

I needed to touch her. I needed to feel her skin against mine. My heart beat frantically against my chest, suddenly awake—suddenly alive. I'd been half a man for the last week and now the rest of me sat crying only a few meters away.

I closed the space between us in a few bounds and then she was there. I cupped her face, drawing her against me, and mashing my lips to her forehead. Her fingers fumbled for my collar, holding me against her. I barely processed the salt on my tongue. I didn't know if it was her tears or mine I was tasting. Not that there was any difference. We were two halves of the same soul.

I didn't pay attention as the others yelled instructions to one another. They could handle this and the inevitable fall-out. Clara was real and in my arms and nothing else mattered.

Pulling away slightly, I drank in her face—the freckles, that dusted her nose, her wide, gray eyes, lips I wanted to feel against mine. But before I could make that dream a reality, we lifted off and she gave a startled yelp that turned into a keening moan. Her hands slipped from my collar to clutch her stomach. My eyes swept over hers finally catching what I'd missed: the hospital gown, the sheen of sweat on her brow, and the slight trail of blood dried on her leg.

"Baby's coming," she grunted, her eyes full of panic.

I could only imagine the fear she'd experienced in the last few days. Now I could see her fraying at the edges. I had to be her strength. I had to help her through this.

I nodded, pressing my lips to her neck and murmuring words I wasn't certain she could hear until she relaxed again in my arms.

Waving for a headset, I took it and spoke directly to Brex, "I assume we're heading into St. Mary's."

"That's the plan, Poor Boy. I'm about to radio in to have the landing pad cleared."

"Make sure her doctor is there and get all the exits sealed off. I don't want any unexpected visitors today," I ordered. No one was coming near my wife without going through me first. Not after what she'd been through. I kept my hands on her, rubbing her back soothingly as I discussed the plan.

"Better call Edward and Belle," Smith's voice broke over the comms.

Yes, Clara would want them there. I pushed aside the flood of guilt I felt at hearing my brother's name. I would talk to him later. I would explain then. He would want to be there now.

"The Bishops?" Brex asked.

"Let's focus on Clara first." I had no doubt that our dramatic arrival at St. Mary's would catch media attention. That meant there was no need to call up her mum. The last thing my wife's blood pressure needed at the moment was Madeline Bishop.

Clara's body went rigid in my arms and I looked down to discover her face twisted in pain. "And Brex? Fly fast."

"Roger," he said. I took off the headset and passed it across the seat, looking up for the first time to see the new addition to our party.

Norris's blue eyes met mine, his face a mask of reassuring calm despite the smeared ash and drawn lines. He looked like he'd been through battle. I didn't bother to question his odd clothing. He was here, and I knew he was the reason Clara was alive and in my arms.

Keeping one arm around her, I stretched the other across to him and he gripped it firmly. I had hundreds of questions for him. They could all wait. I was about to become a father again and judging from Clara's near constant pain, that would be happening soon.

I rearranged her in my arms, helping her rest against me as I supported her weight. I knew she couldn't hear a word I whispered to her over the blades cutting through the air but I kept talking anyway.

"You're so brave. It's nearly over. I'm here. I'm going to

be right here with you." I wrote promises on her skin with words unheard. She felt them. I hoped they gave her strength.

Clara had faced so much. She would overcome this, too.

When we finally touched down on the helicopter pad at St. Mary's, a medical team was waiting. Clara shrank away from them as they tried to help her into a wheelchair.

"I've got it," I called as the blades began to slow.

The nurses looked torn between fighting for their jobs and taking on the King. In the end, they stepped aside.

"Show me the way." I wheeled Clara quickly after them. She reached up, covering my hand with hers, as desperate for the contact as I was. If it was up to me, I would have carried her inside and held her through the entire labor.

"They're prepping the surgery suite," a nurse told me as we made our way out of the lift and down the corridor. "Dr. Ball is on the way to deliver the baby."

"No," Clara moaned. "I want a room. I need to move."

The nurse shot me a panicked look. "How long has she been in labor?"

I didn't have an answer to that question, but I wasn't about to go against my wife's wishes now. I had no idea how she'd been violated during our time apart, but I would do everything I could to empower her from this moment forward. "Get us a room. I'll speak to the doctor."

When we were finally shown into a birthing suite, Clara looked to me. "You and Belle."

This proclamation was followed by an unearthly moan.

I turned on the nurses who'd begun to set up monitors. One had rushed in with an IV. "Clara, they need to prep you for..."

She shook her head. "Baby is coming now."

"Your Majesty," a nurse dared to interject, earning her sharp looks from both of us.

"Out!" I ordered them.

"We can't allow—" the nurse argued.

"Out!" I roared. They didn't dare to disagree.

"Poppet," I said gently. "We're probably going to need the nurses."

Her eyes narrowed, but she finally nodded. "Just give me a minute."

I'd been trying to help her into bed the entire time, but she wasn't having it. Instead, she shucked off the hospital gown, tossing it to the ground with a disgusted whimper. I watched as her abdomen tightened and Clara lunged for the bed railing, bending into the pain.

I didn't know what to do, so I stayed close, rubbing her back, and supporting her. My wife knew what she needed and I wasn't about to question that—not after what she'd been through.

We'd endured another five contractions in various positions when there was a knock on the door. A second later, Belle poked her head inside.

"I was called...oh!" She took in Clara, who was currently leaning against me in a sort of half squat. "Should I get the nurses?"

Clara shook her head, her teeth gritted as she breathed

through another round. Belle came inside and closed the door quickly behind her.

"No one's sure what to do out there," she told me. "Brex and Smith are keeping them away from the door. Are we sure she should..."

She trailed away as Clara let out a blood piercing cry and reached for her. Belle took her best friends hands, the momentary shock wearing off with the contact. Tears began to stream down her face.

She sniffed hard, shaking her head and channeling the stalwart British calm our people called upon in moments of crisis. "Well, let's get this going, shall we?"

Clara shot her a wan smile. "It's going. Oh my god, I think I want to push."

At her words, the hospital door opened and in strolled Dr. Ball, who did a double take at the scene unfolding before him.

"Clara, we need to get you into surgery," he began. "I've been trying to reach Dr. Rolland. We'll want to control..."

I stopped listening to him as I felt Clara shrink in my arms. When I looked to her, her face was wild and desperate. Her hand reached for my collar, clutching it tightly. "Don't let them touch me. Not them. Don't...let...the baby..."

She was trying to tell me something while a contraction complicated things. But the message was clear. She was terrified of him—and there was only one reason why.

My eyes flew to Ball, as fury blazed within me. I

wanted to pin him to the wall and beat him to a bloody pulp.

I released Clara into Belle's keeping and rounded on the doctor, who backed up, his hands flying into the air in surrender. Either he was a very good actor or completely flummoxed as to the cause of Clara's fear. Grabbing him by the lab coat, I dragged him into the hall.

"Watch him," I ordered Brex. "I want him questioned." The nurses who had been waiting in the corridor tried to blend into the wall. "Get another doctor up here and find me someone who can operate on the baby."

I didn't have time for clearer instructions. I shoved Ball in their direction. He'd begun to protest the treatment but otherwise didn't resist. I didn't care what he had to say. I'd seen the pure terror on Clara's face. That made him guilty in my eyes.

When I returned to the room, Clara reached out for me. Hurrying to her, I knelt and allowed her to hold onto my shoulders.

"Dr. Rol—" A contraction halted her and she fought to keep speaking. "Land was....there..."

My eyes flashed to Belle's. I didn't know this doctor, but Clara did.

"It's the neonatal surgeon," Belle said quickly, conveying what Clara could not at the moment. "The one who confirmed the baby's heart condition."

"I doubt he's on his way here," I muttered, doing my best to stay calm as fury ripped through me. A doctor—one she'd known and trusted—had betrayed her. "What about Ball?"

Clara shook her head. "But I...I..."

"I know, poppet." She didn't have to explain. There was no way to be certain Ball hadn't known more about what happened to her, which meant he wasn't about to get near her.

"I think I want to push," she said through clenched teeth.

"Clara, I'm going to get a doctor," Belle said gently. "Not Ball, I promise."

She nodded to her best friend, her teeth beginning to chatter.

"Are you cold, poppet?"

She shook her head. I wanted to take away her pain—to bear it for her. It was driving me crazy to see her like this, and yet, I was proud. She'd fought them. She'd survived. She could do anything.

"X." My name on her lips was a soothing balm but also a plea.

"Tell me what you need." I would do anything for her. I just had to know what to do.

She pulled away, bending over the bed and beginning to sway as Belle reappeared with an older female doctor.

"Doctor Thompson." She came over and shook my head purposefully looking me directly in the eye. "It seems your wife has had a change of heart."

That was a mild way of putting it. "Is it safe for her to have the baby?"

"She seems to be doing just fine." Thompson looks her up and down. "I'd like to check her though."

"Ask her." I wasn't about to give anyone permission to touch her.

"Clara," Dr. Thompson said calmly. "You look like you're ready to have a baby. I'd like to check the baby's heart rate if that's all right. That will make certain that we're safe in proceeding."

Clara nodded, her teeth still clicking together. Thompson meanwhile bent down with her stethoscope. After a few moments, she straightened with a smile. "Sounds beautiful. Would you like me to check you?"

Clara looked at me apprehensively. I wondered how long it would be before she trusted someone to touch her. All I could do was reassure her that I was here. "It's okay."

She nodded, starting to push up onto the bed.

"Don't bother," Thompson stopped her. "You look like you've found a position you like. Stool please."

I was in a daze. This was happening so fast, unlike last time. I slid a stool to Thompson who settled on it like she was about to read the morning paper. Belle and I exchanged glances while Thompson checked the situation.

How far did we allow this to go? If Clara needed an intervention, did either of us have the heart to tell her?

"You are ready to have this baby," Thompson said warmly. "Would you mind if a nurse joined us? Someone I trust?"

She seemed to understand that something out of the ordinary was happening, but rather than take control she was allowing Clara to retain it.

I think we'd found our new family physician.

"Yes," Clara groaned.

"Good, because we're going to need all hands on deck. Would you mind calling for Gillian?" Thompson asked Belle.

Belle did as she was told, her face a mixture of apprehension and excitement. Only a few hours ago, we weren't certain we would ever see Clara again. Now we were about to witness her giving birth.

"We have a neonatal surgeon prepared. Once the cord is cut, we'll need to administer some medications to keep the baby's valve open until we can have surgery." She spoke directly to Clara, laying out each step as she spoke and erasing any room for doubt or fear. "We don't have to cut the cord right away. We'll let you decide."

"You can do that?" I said, slightly awe-struck. Thompson shot me a look that said I was out of my league.

"Yes, for hours. When she's ready, we'll take the next steps," she said pointedly.

I couldn't imagine what trauma the doctor suspected Clara had endured, but she was here for *her* and seemed intent to make that clear.

"But for now, I think you're ready to meet your baby." Thompson turned back to Clara, not bothering to order her onto the bed.

Everything happened in a haze. Clara moved and swayed and moaned. She clung to me, drinking in as much love as I could give her as she worked to bring our child into the world, and then she did it.

He was here.

CHAPTER 25

CLARA

Life changed in an instant. One minute I was ready to tell Alexander that if he even looked at me again I would neuter him, and the next I was clutching a beautiful baby boy. I waited for him to scream, noting with alarm that he was slightly blue and then he opened his mouth and yowled.

Instinct took over, and I brought the baby to my breast as the others helped me into the bed I'd wanted nothing to do with for the last hour. I was suddenly grateful for its existence.

Alexander moved beside me, leaning closer but still keeping his distance. It was oddly shy of him, considering he usually couldn't keep his hands off me.

"Come meet your son," I said softly, adjusting the baby to keep him close while giving his father a better view.

"Hello there, little prince," Alexander whispered. He stared in awe at the miracle we'd been given.

Hours ago, I couldn't have imagined this gift. I'd

thought I would never hold my child. I'd thought Alexander would never meet him. Now we were here—together and complete.

"Elizabeth!" In all of the chaos, I hadn't thought to send for our daughter.

"Shh!" Alexander brushed a lock of hair from my forehead. "She's on her way. Georgia and Brex went to get her."

I had no idea how he'd had the presence of mind to handle all of this, but my man—my strong, capable man—had rolled with every punch and fought beside me. Rawness coated my throat and I blinked against the heat prickling my eyes.

Too late.

It was all too much. It was everything I ever wanted.

"Everything's okay. She's coming," Alexander said, trying to reassure me. He'd mistaken my tears for something else. Guilt? Fear?

Or maybe he hadn't. Even as joy filled me, a dozen new sensations crowded inside me as well. The events of the last few days suddenly hit me. I'd been so focused on keeping my cool and staying alive that I'd never really allowed myself to give in to the fear or hopelessness. Now it hit me like a delayed-release capsule.

"There are things I need to tell you," I choked out as the tears began to flow freely. "You need to know what they did. You need to know..."

I couldn't bring myself to begin. Alexander cast a dark look at Dr. Thompson who was busy wrapping up the final birthing issues. Belle, who'd faded into the background, came near, drawn by my words.

I looked to my best friend, wondering how I could tell her what had happened—who had betrayed us.

"Belle, I need to speak to Edward..." I blubbered, becoming incoherent half-way through. I couldn't talk to him. Not now.

"He'll be here," she said automatically, even as confusion dashed over her face. "I'll go get him."

"Not yet," I stopped her. "We need some time."

"Okay." She smiled, but I noted she hadn't come closer. Was I acting like a crazy person? "Do you mind if I update the others?"

"Please." Alexander nodded, his attention staying on me.

"I'll give you two a few minutes." She hesitated mid-turn. "Call if you need me."

As soon as she was out the door, the dam burst. Up until this moment, I hadn't considered how my story was going to hurt the people in my life. "X, I have to tell you...who..."

"It can wait, poppet," he murmured. He placed a gentle hand on my shoulder—an anchor to remind that he was here. I had nothing to fear.

But it wasn't just about what they'd done. No one knew the extent of the havoc they'd wreaked.

No one knew their plan.

No one knew about David.

Cold suspicion broke over me as the nurse tried to come over for the baby. Would they have just let me go? What if this was their back-up plan? What if the moment I handed him over, they planned to whisk him away?

Dr. Rolland hadn't come when called, which was smart. Regardless of the bullshit excuse that he only cared about the baby, that man was never going near my child. But could MI-18 find another doctor? Their whole plan was built around taking him from us.

"I just need to perform a few tests, ma'am," the nurse said with a syrupy smile.

I held him away as my body began to shake.

"Is she okay?" Alexander asked in alarm as the tremors grew worse.

"It's completely normal," Dr. Thompson assured him. "Her body's endured a lot. Let's get her wrapped up."

"And the baby?" Alexander's eyes darted to me.

"He's looking fine to me. I heard his lungs." Thompson chuckled as she unfolded a blanket and eased it around me. "We can clean him up in a bit. I will need to administer some medicine and listen to his heart, Clara. But you may hold him."

"But he needs surgery," I whispered. I knew I couldn't keep him in my arms forever. It was the painful truth of being a mother: eventually you had to let your child go. But this wasn't a simple matter of not being ready. No one realized the danger he might be in.

"Yes," Thompson said slowly, "but we don't need to rush. This time is important for both of you. When the neonatal surgeon arrives, we'll discuss the next steps. For now, take some time getting to know your son."

A weight lifted off my shoulders, but I couldn't quite ignore the dread still lingering inside me. I was delaying the inevitable. I wouldn't be able to keep him with me. Still, he was here now and that was enough.

Alexander sat carefully on the edge of the bed and reached a tentative hand towards him.

"Go on, X," I urged him. I appreciated his cautious respect, but he was the only person I didn't mind touching our son.

"Change your mind on the name?" he asked, brushing the baby's cheek with reverence.

"Not unless you have." An unexpected bubble of laughter burst out of me. I'd gone from sobbing to laughing in the pan of a minute. I was losing my mind.

"Then hello there, William." Alexander's hand cupped his head and the baby turned slightly like he liked the attention before returning to my breast.

"Now we only have twenty more to choose from," I said dryly. As soon as I spoke my good mood evaporated. We'd discussed the baby's middle names and how to best pay tribute to the other men of our family. Now I couldn't bear thinking of those names and all the sorrow that accompanied them.

Albert. The man who'd given his life to save his son's, but left a complicated web behind him. The man who had made me feel small and little and unwanted. The man who might have been protecting us from this all along. Could I allow my son to carry that moniker? Could I handle its weight?

Edward. The brother I'd never had. My best friend. My confidant. The best of us. He was the person I'd most wanted to honor, but now it hurt to think of him. Not because my feelings toward him had changed, but because of the terrible secret I carried.

Harold. My father's name and the one I'd been most worried about now felt like a safe choice.

And then there was David. I could barely bring myself to think his name.

"We have time." Alexander leaned over and kissed me. "Make them wait a few days. Make them wait a month. It will drive the bookies crazy."

I tried to smile but it came out lopsided. My heart wasn't in it.

Alexander seemed to sense this. He stayed close while giving me space, allowing the doctor and nurse to finish the final assessments.

When Dr. Thompson came to listen to William's heart, I reluctantly turned him away from me.

She bent her gray head down and listened intently, her face remaining composed. It was too perfect. No reaction.

Something was wrong.

"What is it?" I asked, unwilling to sit and wait for her to deliver the bad news. I'd been preparing mentally for this since I'd found out about William's heart condition, but the truth was that nothing could ever prepare you for a sick child.

I was his mother. It was my job to protect him. He'd grown inside me, and no matter how much reason and common sense was laid at my feet, I felt responsible. Maybe I could have done more. Maybe I was to blame.

"I think it would be a good idea to have the surgeon come in sooner." She straightened, her lips a flat line.

"We should have had the c-section," I said as guilt shook me.

"That doesn't matter." She waved off the idea with such dismissal that it almost made me feel better. "And he's here now, but I do believe the valve will need attention sooner rather than later. I'll give you two a few moments."

She disappeared with the nurse, giving us our first real moment of alone time. I sighed into the feeling. This was where I belonged with Alexander in our own world. When I looked up, I found his lashes wet.

"Hey, X. How are you doing?" He'd been so concerned with me that I hadn't asked him.

"Does that matter?" He forced a crooked grin that didn't quite match him anymore. There had been a time when that wicked smirk could stop any conversation, no matter how serious, and get me thinking about something else. But since that was the *last* thing I felt like thinking about at the moment, it didn't work now.

"It matters to me." With the baby sleeping peacefully on my chest, I finally took one hand off William and placed it over my husband's.

"I thought I'd lost you," he whispered, his eyes focused on our clasped hands.

"You didn't." It was a simple reminder but one we both needed. We'd walked through hell and we'd come out the other side. But there were burns that would take time to heal. We could only start that process together.

"We need to talk," I continued, feeling more comfortable now that we were alone. "I have to tell you something...about David."

"I know," he said quickly.

"You do?"

"We saw him." He hesitated, and I could see he was holding something back.

Was he trying to save the bad news until later? I already knew almost everything I needed to know. That David was a traitor. That Norris had shot him. The only mystery was how I was going to tell Edward what had happened.

I didn't know how I was going to break my best friend's heart.

"Norris shot him. He's dead," I said in a soft voice, needing him to know that I understood the weight of what happened. "He was helping them—whoever they were. They planned to take the baby."

"We don't need to talk about this now," Alexander stopped me. "You shouldn't have to relive it."

I understood. Part of me wanted to take him up on the offer, but deep down I knew I couldn't escape this.

"Clara," he continued, "there's something you need to know." Alexander's jaw tightened as though he wanted to hold back the words. "David was alive when I found him."

"Was?" I repeated the most significant word in that sentence. David was alive? He'd lived? I didn't know how to feel about that.

"Was," Alexander said again. "He's not anymore."

I stared at my husband, trying to process what he was saying. William shifted on my chest, turning his face with sudden, undeniable interest. I repositioned him while the weight of Alexander's confession snack through me like lead.

"I didn't think." Alexander's voice trembled as he spoke. This wasn't the first man he'd killed. He'd been to war. But this was different, and we both knew it. "I didn't even think. When I realized what he did...I shot him."

And somewhere through the grief and fear and love and anger swimming inside me, I knew exactly how I felt about what he'd done. "Good."

CHAPTER 26

ALEXANDER

I blinked, momentarily stunned by Clara's reaction. I'd never seen such bald hatred on her face, but before I could ask for more details—even though I'd promised I wouldn't—the door to her room opened.

Dr. Thompson entered, followed by a man I didn't recognise. Both of them were studying me. I knew Dr. Thompson had gotten the wrong impression during labor. It seemed I was going to have to prove to them that my wife had no reason to fear me. That was easier said than done.

"Dr. Gilroy is here," Thompson announced, "and he'd like to take a look at the baby."

Clara released him to the doctor's care reluctantly, her eyes darting between the baby and the man. I didn't know how to allay her fears. The truth was that I had been caught off guard. That mistake had nearly cost us everything. I was the reason she was scared now. How could I ever convince her that I would never allow that to happen again?

"Stay with him," Clara urged me, her exhaustion beginning to show.

"Actually, I'd like to speak with your husband." Dr. Thompson didn't care that I was king—that much was obvious. She had a bone to pick with me.

"I'll get Belle," I promised her.

Belle hurried in from the hall as soon as I asked for her. None of my team had strayed farther than the corridor. We must have made the hospital nervous. Most of us look like we'd just walked out of a war zone. Then there was the hovering. The tension outside the delivery room was palpable. No wonder the doctor was on edge.

"She wants someone to stay with the baby," I explained to Belle under my breath, so curious ears didn't overhear. "She's scared someone will take him, but I need to speak with Dr. Thompson."

Belle swallowed hard, digesting this news. I didn't know how much Smith had managed to relay to her about today's events, but there was a lot the rest of my team didn't know. Now wasn't the time to fill them in.

"Edward's on his way," Belle told me as we headed back inside. "He can't reach David."

Guilt pressed against my chest. I knew what she didn't —what my brother didn't. There would be no reaching David again. Clara might have absolved me for my part in his death, but I had not.

I had no idea if my brother ever would.

I gave her a terse nod, hoping she wouldn't bring it up again—not in front of Clara.

Belle beamed at her best friend and darted over to where the surgeon was examining the baby on a nearby cart. I had to hand it to her. She knew things had gone terribly wrong, but she was putting on the best show of any of us.

"Doctor," I addressed Thompson, motioning for her to join me in the corner. It wasn't exactly private, but there was no need to keep anything from Clara and my wife would feel better knowing I was here.

"I suppose you can guess what we need to speak about. Normally, I would ask a woman directly, but I'm not certain I would get a straight answer from your wife. She obviously lives in fear." She leveled a beady gaze at me.

It took all my self-control not to snap. This was understandable. She had misinterpreted the situation. Given how carefully we'd controlled news of Clara's abduction, I couldn't blame her for that. "It's not what you think."

"I hear that a lot." She crossed her arms, obviously preparing for a fight.

It was going to be hard to stay cool-headed if she wasn't going to listen. "My men. This." I pointed to my strange attire. "Someone attempted to take the baby."

"But the baby…" She trailed away as she began to put this together.

"Clara was in labor when we found her." I kept my voice low. "I assume I have doctor patient privilege."

I should have thought of that first.

She nodded, a humourless smile playing at her lips. "You could also order me not to speak."

"You don't seem like the type to take orders," I admitted.

"Neither does your wife." She looked over to Clara who was watching us from the bed. "She'll need to speak with someone."

"She will." I would do every thing in my power to help her heal from this, and I would make certain it never happened again.

"I wish it wasn't necessary to remove the baby, but you should know, I think the surgery will need to be performed today." She looked genuinely apologetic to deliver another blow.

"I understand." I tilted my head toward the hospital bed. "I'd like to check on her now."

"Of course." She hesitated. "And I'm sorry, Your Majesty."

"Alexander," I prompted her. "No need to apologise. I will never fault someone for trying to protect her."

When I returned to Clara's side, she clutched my hand.

"Don't worry." I stroked her palm, wishing I could do more to comfort her. "I'm right here. I'm not going anywhere."

Clara's eyes snapped open. "Like hell you aren't. You're going to stay with the baby. He needs the surgery, doesn't he?"

I nodded.

"Then you need to be with him. Don't let him out of your sight." Panic coated her words and I knew that she wasn't going to relax about this.

That left me in an awful position. After days of trying

to find her, I didn't want to let Clara out of my sight. It felt as though she might vanish into thin air again. But I also knew that right now she needed me to be where she couldn't be. Staying with her might make me feel better, but she would be a nervous wreck. I couldn't fault her for that.

"I'll be fine," she said, seeming to sense my dilemma. "Belle will be with me."

Belle turned at the sound of her name and nodded. I wondered how much of our conversation, she'd overheard.

"Promise me, X," she demanded.

It was a promise I had to make.

FOR SANITARY REASONS, I WASN'T ALLOWED IN THE actual operating room, but they were able to find one with a theatre typically reserved for student observations. I had promised Clara I would watch him every second, and I'd walked him to the door, left Brex parked in front of it, and immediately entered the observation area. Still, I couldn't quite handle the site of my hours-old son laying limp on an operating table while the doctors worked to fix his heart.

This wasn't the natural order of things. It should have been me lying there, not my child.

"May I join you?" Norris asked from the entrance.

I hadn't let myself think about Norris during his absence. I hadn't dared hope that both of them would be returned to me. Now, I felt guilty for focusing almost solely on retrieving Clara. I wasn't sure I deserved having them both safe.

"You're quiet," he noted, coming to stand beside me at the window. "Of course, this must be difficult for you."

It took me a few more minutes to speak. We watched the operation in mute companionship, each comforted and overwhelmed by each other's presence.

"I thought you were dead," I finally said in a voice that sounded too distant to be my own. I had thought it, but I hadn't allowed myself to feel it. Now those reactions collided, fusing into a strangely frustrated feeling.

"I probably should be," he admitted. "It was MI-18."

I nodded. "We figured that out."

I wanted to tell him everything I knew, but something held me back. I had questions for Norris. There wasn't a bone in my body that suspected him of anything, but I needed to see this more clearly and I could only do that through his eyes.

"I don't know what Clara's told you," he began.

"I kept making her stop. She needs to rest." I stood by that decision. We couldn't pretend this hadn't happened, but there were more important things at the moment. The monitor measuring my son's heartbeat, for instance. My eyes were glued to it as we spoke.

"It was an ambush," he explained, walking me through the night's events. His story matched up with what we'd assumed. "I never saw them. I let my guard down. Alexander, I'm sorry. Forgive me."

"There's nothing to forgive." My words were thick. I never thought I'd speak to my old friend again. Now he felt like he had to apologise. "I knew you would protect her with your life."

"I wasn't paying enough attention." He shook his head, obviously unable to forgive himself so easily. "I tried to warn her. When I woke up, they tried to convince me that I'd been hospitalised and was in custody for her disappearance. They claimed you had ordered it."

My eyebrow shot up. "They must not know me very well."

"Or me," he agreed. "I knew it was a lie. But I also knew that meant they had Clara. It was all a ruse anyway. They were after something else."

I stared at the prize they'd tried to claim through the glass: an innocent life. Why? For what purpose? To hurt me? To bring me to my knees? How could I live with myself knowing I'd placed my family in this danger? How would I ever move forward?

"The baby," I murmured. "Clara said they wanted the baby. I don't understand why."

"I think I do," he said slowly, "but it's only a hunch."

"Why?" His hunches were almost always fact. It's why they had kept him from me during this. The manhunt would have lasted hours rather than days if he'd been by my side.

"I started to suspect when I stumbled on something, but I knew when I saw David. I assume you know about your sister."

I nodded. We'd figured out that Sarah had been under their control for years while we thought she was in a coma. I didn't understand that either, but I had a better idea. "She says they aren't in contact. We're still investigating whether she can be trusted or if she's acting as a mole."

"She's not," he said grimly. "I think they kept her in the dark. Possibly, they thought they could turn her to their cause, unseat your place in line, and put her on the throne."

That made a sort of horrific sense. "But why take Clara? Why not just kill me?"

"They tried, and you survived. We've known for a long time there was more to Daniel's assassination attempt. I'm afraid that was only the beginning."

"Was this the end?" I asked knowing he couldn't offer me a comforting answer.

Norris didn't try to placate me. "I doubt it, but know we know what we're up against. Who we're up against."

"So they gave up on Sarah because Clara had Elizabeth," I said. None of this led to why they'd taken her now and why they wanted my son.

"I think they found she was too old to manipulate. That's why they put David into play," he said, his eyes darting over to me. "I must confess something. I killed him. He was trying to hurt Clara."

My eyes flickered from the operating table to the look of anguish on his face. At least, this was one sin I could absolve him from. "No, you didn't. I did."

"How?" Norris asked in shock.

"He was alive. I found him and when I realized..." I shook my head. I'd acted rashly but I still wasn't certain I'd made the wrong choice.

"No one could blame you," Norris said firmly.

"Edward could." I tried to imagine what I would do if my brother took Clara's life. There would be no forgiveness. There would be no peace. Nothing would ever be the same. I knew that.

"I will take the blame," Norris decided. "A brother shouldn't bear that burden."

"I'll bear it all the same," I said. "I can't lie to him. I have to tell him." I'd learned that lying to someone you loved could destroy everything. I couldn't pretend or make up a story. I had to come clean and face the consequences.

"There's something else you should know. I expect it was part of the plan." Norris cleared his throat, searching for words that wouldn't come.

The pause gave me time to remember the papers I'd stolen from the file during our raid. I pulled them out and opened them. "I found these. It seems like they were doing testing on you. Sarah said they did the same on her. I haven't asked Clara yet. What are they doing? Why? Do you have any idea?"

"That makes sense." He turned toward me, drawing my attention for a moment from my child. "I never wanted you to find this out. I promised her I would keep a secret until the day I died. It was our secret—the one bit of happiness your father could never take from us."

My mouth went dry. I stared down at the strange diagrams clearly labeled with his name and matched up with two other sets.

"Your mother and I..." He took a steadying breath before plunging on. "We fell in love. We were never certain. There were never any tests, but Elizabeta believed that Sarah was my daughter."

I stared at him, every thought in my head halting at once.

"We suspected Edward was my child as well. Those tests appear to confirm it." He hung his head. For the first time in my life, Norris couldn't meet my eyes.

But I wasn't angry at him. Shocked? Yes. Full of questions? Obviously. This man had been like a father to me more so than my own had ever been. "And me?"

He looked a little sad as he answered. "I've always looked at you like a son, but I didn't meet your mother until after you were born. You are the only one of Albert's children with a legitimate claim to the throne."

A curious mix of disappointment and understanding settled over me. Suddenly, so many things made sense. My father's callous treatment of my siblings. His hatred of me. It must have killed him to see me with the man who'd stolen his wife—but only if he knew. "Did Albert...?"

"Yes and no. He knew about the affair. He had plenty of his own. It didn't bother him until Sarah was born. He suspected what Elizabeta knew," Norris said simply. "We guarded that knowledge with our lives."

"And somehow MI-18 found out about it." It was a lot to process in a day that was already full of overwhelming events.

"I'll tender my resignation tomorrow. Today I would like to watch over your family," he said quietly.

"Like hell you will," I roared. "I can't blame you for being a man. You were a better father to me than he ever was. This isn't a job. You can't quit family—and you are family."

We would be forced to face this later. We'd have to confront the harsh reality of what this meant to who we were and how it would affect the ones we loved. But nothing changed the simple fact that family was built through love, not blood. Stepping toward him, I embraced him as a father, as a friend, as family.

CHAPTER 27

CLARA

My family arrived the following morning with fanfare that I could hear from the hallway. I didn't know who told them we were here—it was probably BBC One. I'd opted to stay through the night to be close to William and receive extra IV fluids. Now I wished I was home where I could avoid the spectacle. Even Madeline Bishop couldn't get into the palace if I told her no.

"Bollocks," Alexander muttered from the chair, woken from his nap. He'd only been sleeping for an hour while Brex and Norris guarded the neonatal unit. The hospital was working on setting up a private room so we could all be together. I'd been aching to hold William, having only been allowed to touch him with protective gloves since the surgery. Now I was grateful we hadn't been moved to our space yet. "Is that your mum?"

"I fear it is." He was close enough that I could reach over and tousle his hair. When he wasn't with William, he was always near enough to touch me. He wanted me at arm's length so he could hold on if needed.

"Should I send them away?" Alexander turned worried eyes on me. He was still deferring to my desires, which was so unlike him that it left me flustered.

I knew he was trying to give me back the perception of control, but wasn't that all any of us ever had? The illusion that we called the shots? The last few days had taught me that wasn't the case and regardless of how he treated me now, I'd learned that lesson the hard way.

"Poppet?" he prompted when I didn't answer.

"Might as well get it over with." Some things simply had to be seen through. I'd survived child labor. I could survive seeing my family. Alexander stood to move to the door and I panicked. "I don't want them to know what happened!"

A muscle ticked in his jaw, but he nodded. He'd told the doctor some of the last week's events because she'd forced him to with her questions. There was no reason that anyone else needed to know.

Alexander had barely stepped through the doorway when the Bishops burst in. It was such an ordinary thing—balloons and presents and smiles—that I burst into tears.

My mother stopped in her tracks, frozen by my response. Then her eyes slowly swept the room. I knew what she was looking for and what she wouldn't find. I didn't have the energy to explain.

"Where's the baby?" she asked, her voice an octave higher than normal.

"Madeline." Alexander stepped in to handle the situation before it became a scene. "As I started to say, I need to speak with you all for a moment. Perhaps, the hall…"

"Nonsense. My daughter is clearly upset. No one even called us to let us know the baby was born." She fanned herself, casting concerned glances at me with eyes that looked alarmingly wet as well. "What is going on? I'm not leaving her."

"The baby needed a special surgery," Alexander kept his voice low in an effort to encourage her to do the same. I doubted that she'd bite on that. "He is in the neonatal unit and can't have visitors."

"I can't see my grandchild?" Madeline's mouth dropped in horror. Behind her my father was doing a remarkable impression of a coat rack for all the emotion he was showing. "Wait! It's a boy?"

Her energy shifted immediately and she turned delighted eyes on her husband. "A boy, Harold!"

"I heard," he said flatly. He glanced to me. "Would you like us to leave?"

It was my father's natural ability to know when his wife was being too much. He coddled her and guided her as best he could.

"Stay." I wiped my eyes and then quickly tacked on, "For a few minutes."

I could use the distraction as long as the conversation steered away from the baby's condition.

Either my mother understood this or she was easily distracted, because instead of insisting on more details, she started to suggest names.

"He already has a name, Mom," I stopped her. "William."

"William," she repeated it like she was trying it on. It was impossible to tell if she approved. "And the other names?"

My husband sensing this was a topic likely to occupy her took the hit. "We haven't decided."

"Oh well, let's see."

Alexander shot me a long-suffering look over her shoulder as she launched into a list of what were no doubt the current favorites at the polls.

When the door opened a few minutes later, my sister's dark head peeked in. "Can we join you?"

I nodded quickly. Lola was even better at keeping our mother in check. But to my surprise, she wasn't alone. Anders loped in behind her carrying a bouquet of flowers.

"Give her the flowers," Lola ordered him, planting her hands on her hips. She looked powerful in a striking red sheath dress that dared anyone to question her.

But Anders seemed unimpressed.

"I know how to bring a woman flowers," he muttered, glaring at her. I could see that my plan to engage my sister's help in readying Anders for the increased scrutiny he would face as a member of the royal family was going over like a bad date.

"Thanks." Alexander intercepted them before the moment could become more awkward.

"Can we see the baby?" Madeline asked.

"Only from an observation window." I knew Alexander wasn't going to budge on this point. We both wanted

William to endure as little stress as possible while he recovered.

"That's fine." Madeline hooked her arm through my father's and marched toward the door. "Lola?"

My sister looked between me and Anders like she was hoping for an out. The issue was that I wanted her there, making sure our mom didn't make a scene.

"I should..." Alexander looked torn between overseeing this visit and staying with me.

"Anders will be here," I reassured him. It was strange to consider that would probably ease his concerns given how he'd once felt about his half-brother.

"Georgia's in the hall," Alexander reminded me. I heard him launch into the rules—ones I suspected he was making up—as he led them away.

"How are you?" Anders asked softly, placing the flowers on the table next to my bed.

"I don't want to talk about it." He hadn't been here for the brief explanation of what had happened, but he wasn't one to pry. "How are you?"

"You really want to know?" His mouth quirked into a frown. "Your sister is driving me nuts!"

I bit back a laugh and tried to look sympathetic.

"She's thrown out half my clothes, insists on taking me to fancy dinners to practice my etiquette"—he wiggled his pinky with a glare that could freeze hell—"and she keeps talking about a plant-based diet. I don't mind some veg with my rashers, but I'm not about to become a bloody vegan."

Lola had clearly gotten under his skin, and while I felt slightly guilty for finding it funny, I hadn't felt this light in days. I let him continue his rant, pleased to see the world through his eyes for a few minutes.

When Alexander reappeared with my family in tow, he announced that visiting hours were over. "Clara needs to feed the baby and well, obviously..."

I had no idea what magic he'd worked on my mother, but she nodded reverently. Dashing over, she gave me a quick hug.

"We'll visit tomorrow," she promised.

I tried to hide my cringe. Lola and dad shook their heads behind my back. They'd keep her at bay now that they knew the seriousness of the situation. After all the hugs, I got up, tightening my robe around me as I slid my feet into a pair of hospital shoes for the long walk to the NICU. The weight that had lifted listening to Anders's rant began to descend again.

Alexander held out his hand and I instantly felt lighter. There was nothing we couldn't face together. We were alive and safe and we would see this through.

In the hall, Georgia glanced up from a Star magazine, a smug look on her face. "You already made the papers." She waved it at me. "They said you're still here getting a tummy tuck and boob job."

Out of all the people who'd saved me yesterday, she was doing the best job of acting normally. Sometimes I even wondered if it was an act. But something else had shifted between us.

She was friendly but distant. The closeness I'd began to feel to her was absent.

"They're going to be disappointed," I said dryly. I glanced at Alexander. "Give me a minute."

He nodded, taking a few steps down the hall.

"Can we talk?" I asked her.

She shrugged and tossed the magazine on a table.

"Shoot." The second the word left her mouth, her casual veneer cracked. "I'm sorry. That was a terrible choice of words."

"You said yourself that you're not very good at this friend thing," I reminded her. "Look, I just wanted to say thanks."

"Thanks?" she repeated. "Clara, none of this would have happened if I'd stayed with you like I was supposed to."

"You were angry." And she'd had a right to be. But she was also putting too much pressure on herself. "They got through Norris. I mean..."

"Are you saying they could have got through me?" Her lips formed a perfect pout. "Now you're the shitty friend."

"I'm just glad nothing happened to you," I said quietly. I didn't want to press my luck further. She would blame herself and hide it beneath her tough exterior. I was beginning to understand Georgia Kincaid, even if I felt like I barely knew her.

She blinked, her eyes finding the ground, and then she stood. "Same."

It was an awkward hug, but it was a start.

"Go see your kid," she said, swiping at her eyes as she turned away.

Alexander was waiting near the end of the hall and to

my surprise, we turned in the direction opposite the neonatal unit. "The room is set up," he explained as we approached a private hospital suite.

We hadn't bothered to move from the delivery room yesterday, knowing it would just mean another move eventually. That had left us with a less than comfortable situation, but neither of us complained. The recovery room was much better, especially because a tiny private NICU had been set up in one half of the room.

Norris sat beside the incubator, both hands on his lap, and his eyes on our son. As soon as he saw me, he stood so I could take the chair.

"I'll give you privacy."

It took the help of the nurse to arrange William for his feed given the number of tubes and monitors he was attached to, but despite his early birth, he latched on easily.

Alexander stood in the shadows and watched us, his face unreadable. My eyes danced between our fragile infant and my husband until I couldn't stand the silence anymore.

"What are you thinking?" I called over to him.

He didn't come any closer and when he spoke, my heart began to beat wildly. Something was wrong. I wasn't going to like what he had to say.

"I'm wondering how to keep you safe. I thought I knew, and now..." I heard his sharp inhale. "I can't keep you safe. With all my resources and all my security, I still lost you."

"You didn't lose me," I reminded him. He needed to see that. He needed to stop allowing the darkness to pull him back under. "I'm right here."

"There is a way, poppet, but you aren't going to like it." His voice was so low that I hoped I was imagining it.

"Don't," I commanded him. I couldn't do this. Not now. Not after everything.

But his solution wasn't what I expected.

"I need to abdicate," he said at last.

CHAPTER 28

ALEXANDER

Elizabeth peered across the room from Clara's bed, nearly toppling over in an attempt to get a peek at her baby brother. It was the closest we'd allow her to get for the time being, but it felt wrong leaving her out. I needed my family around me right now. I needed to see clearly what mattered most.

Clara wouldn't share her thoughts on my plan. In fact, she'd been mostly silent since I told her that I meant to abdicate. It wasn't as though there were other options. MI-18 had backed us into a corner, and despite gathering information from Norris and Clara, we had very little to go on.

I'd been unwilling to leave the hospital while my son was in recovery, which left sweeping the remains of Windsmoor to my team.

When Brex knocked on the door, his face was drawn and haggard. He shook his head as I stepped into the hall to join them.

The hospital had been incredibly accommodating, basically clearing out a wing for our use. Then again, it was to be expected. Not that I would enjoy perks like that for much longer.

"Nothing," he said solemnly. "They destroyed it all."

I fell back against the wall. I'd expected it, but it didn't make it any easier to hear. Not after what they'd done to Clara.

"David?" I asked quietly. My brother had been by to visit but he hadn't stayed after confessing that he couldn't reach his husband.

"His body was gone," Smith told me. "When you're ready we can send a team in to identify human remains on sight. But there wasn't much."

The girl I'd found would be among them. I hoped that whoever she was, we could give her family closure. Not that we could tell them the truth.

"And it's still secure?" I asked.

The three of them went silent.

It had been a lot to hope for that the burning down of a royal estate would go unnoticed.

"We've issued a no-fly order over the site. Of course, with the protections in place for private property, it's unlikely anyone will dare," Brex said, but I could tell that was the first and last bit of good news.

"But the media has the area surrounded," Georgia added. "We should issue a statement about it—and this."

That was her delicate way of telling me the hospital was ground zero for the press as well.

It wasn't surprising. We'd offered no news about the baby's birth. The fact that Clara's first birth had been via cesarean bought us some time. No one expected her to make an appearance yet. But there would be no presentation of the baby this time. No fanfare. Our son's welfare trumped public interest.

"There's something we should talk about." I lowered my voice. Despite the privacy afforded us, I knew better than most that some subjects had to be carefully handled. "I've been trying to think of a way to stop this and with nothing to go on..."

"We'll keep looking," Georgia said fiercely. She elbowed Brex and he nodded in agreement.

"I know you will, but there might be an easier solution." I took a deep breath, uncertain how they'd react. "They're only interested in me because I'm King."

From all the clues we'd pieced together that had become obvious.

"We can't do anything about that, Poor Boy." Brex looked at me like I was off my nut.

"Can't we?" I said grimly.

"Are you talking abdication?" Smith wasn't one to mince words. "I'm no fan of the throne—present company mostly excluded—but I don't see how that solves our problems."

"Who would take the throne?" Georgia asked. "Sarah? She can't handle it."

I shook my head. I hadn't told them the truth about her father yet.

"Edward?" Brex asked. "That would be throwing him into the deep end."

It was an issue I hadn't really considered. If Clara and I

renounced our claim to the throne and our children's claim, the line of succession would have to pass to someone. But MI-18 knew that Albert wasn't Sarah or Edward's father, and I had no doubt that fact wouldn't stay secret for long.

That would leave the throne to Henry. I wasn't sure he would appreciate it. There was also legitimising Anders, who would hate me forever.

"I think you have a lot to think about," Smith said. "Let us worry about Windsmoor."

Taking that off my plate was the least I could do.

Ducking back into the suite, I found Clara curled up asleep with Elizabeth. I watched my wife and daughter for a moment. Would I be protecting them by turning over the crown? That was what really mattered. Parliament could sort out who to name as the bloody monarch.

The trouble was that I knew it wasn't that simple.

Norris was sitting vigil next to William's incubator and I joined him.

"Something on your mind?" He knew me too well, which meant there was no reason to beat around the bush.

"I told Clara I want to abdicate. It's the only way I can think that will protect them." I looked over to my wife and daughter's sleeping forms.

"But you're not sure it will be enough," he guessed. Norris had a way of seeing through to the heart of the problem. The truth was that the line of succession wasn't what made me hesitate.

I nodded. "I have resources now that I won't have if..."

"But those resources failed you," Norris added quietly.

"I'm not angry." I really wasn't. Not at my team. Not at

my people. Not even myself. We'd been out-maneuvered. It was a simple fact and one I needed to face. I didn't have the energy to be angry. I was too tired.

"I know, but it puts you in an impossible position." He studied me for a moment, then glanced to my son. "He'll have your life. Your daughter will. It's a life of duty but also privilege."

I knew that better than anyone. I'd fought it for so long that I'd begun to wonder if I'd ever really accepted my role.

"There are many things we don't control in life," he said. "Our parents, for one. Your parentage took a great deal of choice from you. I don't think you've ever forgiven them for that."

"Maybe I haven't." My tongue was dry in my mouth. Was that the real obstacle that had stood between me and my father for all those years? Had I blamed him for something neither of us could control? "Will my children feel the same?"

"Only if you doom them to." Norris shook his head. "Albert was a hard man. He protected people by driving them away. He put up walls instead of building bridges."

"Sounds like someone I know," I muttered. I was more like him than I cared to admit. I'd pushed Clara away again and again, deciding what was best for her. I'd acted without consulting my family. I'd distanced myself just as he had.

"You have something your father never had." Norris looked to Clara. "A woman who loves you more than you can love yourself."

I felt the same way about her. "I don't deserve her. Is that how my father lost my mother?"

My father had loved my mother deeply. I'd never doubted that, but I'd never understood their relationship either. I felt like a cad asking Norris, but he didn't seem to mind.

"He lost her because he didn't deserve her. He cheated. He lied. Perhaps it was to protect her, but it pushed her away." Norris leaned forward and stared me down. "Your love for Clara is nothing like that. Don't doubt true love. Have faith in it."

"And that will save me?" I asked. I needed to know it could. I needed to know that, regardless of what I chose, I could forge a different path with my children.

He smiled slightly, his eyes growing sad. "It saved me."

"Hey." The sound of my brother's voice startled me, and I nearly dropped the tea bag I was holding. Clara needed a pick-me-up and despite her strong affinity for coffee, I knew that tea was what she needed.

I wasn't prepared to speak with Edward alone. So far there had been a crush of people surrounding us every time he'd popped in. It had saved Clara and I from facing him. "Tea?"

"Were you expecting me?" He looked at the cup and screwed up his face. "Obviously not. I don't drink darjeeling—neither does your wife.

Frowning, I dumped it out. "Good to know."

"She really would have rather have coffee, even if she is married to the King," he said dryly. Edward's sense of humour was intact but fraying at the edges. Normally, he looked like he'd stepped out of a magazine. Today his shirt was rumpled, his sleeves rolled up, and his hair a tangled mess. He caught me staring and sighed. "I look that bad, don't I?"

I had a choice to make. It would be easy to ask about David and feign ignorance. But that wouldn't change the past. "David?"

"There's been no word." Edward strolled over to the lounge chair and sank in to it looking defeated.

"I haven't had a chance to talk to you," I began slowly, wondering how this would play out.

"You've had a lot on your plate. David will turn up. The important thing is that Clara is safe." The surety of his words didn't quite cover the tremble in his voice.

"Edward?" How did I tell him this? Where did I begin?

He buried his head in his hands but the action didn't quite cover his muffled sobs. I wished I could say something to comfort him, but that wasn't my job today.

"When Clara was taken," I said in a soft voice, "we only discovered a few of her captors."

Edward's face twisted toward me, confusion swimming in his tear-stained eyes. Slowly, I saw the gears begin to turn. "What does this have to do with David?"

"Everything," I confessed.

"Oh god." Edward gripped his knees, beginning to tremble. He stood, shaking his head, an accusation flung in my direction. "You're wrong."

"I'm not. I saw him. He told me." I wasn't certain if this was the harder bit of news. What I had to tell him next should be the worst, but somehow I knew it wasn't. I couldn't imagine finding out the person I loved had betrayed me and my family.

Clara had begun to share more details, repeating the reasons David had given her for his actions. She was convinced he'd loved Edward. Neither of us felt it made up for what he'd done.

"Where is he?" Edward sounded hollow as though he was answering automatically. "Prison? Custody?"

I couldn't bring myself to answer. I couldn't bring myself to look at him.

"Alex." Edward's voice peaked, his breath beginning to speed up. "Where is he?"

I forced myself to meet his eyes. I forced myself to confront what I'd done. "I'm sorry. I killed him."

Edward didn't move. He stared at me like I hadn't spoken at all.

I wanted to tell him I had no choice, but that was a lie. I'd decided to face my actions. "He hurt her. He betrayed us."

It might not be enough of an explanation, but it was all I could offer now. I wasn't sure he could process more as it was.

But Edward didn't ask any questions. He didn't scream. He'd just stared blankly at me, which was somehow worse, until he finally turned and walked away, leaving me there with my guilt and an empty cup of tea.

"Where's my tea?" Clara asked when I returned to the suite. We were alone for the time being with William. Aunt Belle had arrived to take Elizabeth home for a few hours so we could focus on the baby. It was difficult enough to care for an infant without a bundle of toddler energy rocketing about.

"I was informed you don't like darjeeling," I said, dumping the cup in the trash at the door. I had no idea why I'd carried it all the way back here. Maybe some things were harder to let go of than others.

"What happened?" Clara sat up her seat, studying me anxiously.

"I spoke with Edward." I didn't have to say more.

Clara's hand flew to her mouth. "Oh my God. Where is he? Is he here? I should find him."

"He left. I don't know." I ran my hands through my hair, trying to understand my sudden need for brutal honesty. What purpose had it served to tell him the truth? "Why didn't I lie? Fake an accident?"

"Because that's what your father would have done," she said softly.

"I broke his heart." I hated myself for hurting my brother this way. Why had Smith given me that gun? Why hadn't I thought about what would happen?

"David broke his heart. He knew what he was doing," she corrected me.

"I pulled the trigger." Nothing would change that.

"And he walked into that room." Clara shook her head. "I'm not asking you to get over it. I don't know if you can. I don't know if I can. But he made his choice. Believe me, I gave him a chance to change his mind. Did you talk to him about abdication?"

"No. It didn't seem important." Given that was all we'd

discussed the last two days, it seemed crazy. "Plus, it will only raise more questions."

I couldn't give up the throne without speaking to my siblings, but that meant coming clean to them about Norris. I wasn't certain it was the right time.

"Maybe it isn't important." Clara had allowed me to do most of the talking about what it would mean if we stepped down. This was the first time she'd expressed an opinion.

"What does that mean, poppet?" I asked.

"It's not my choice, X."

"Yes, it is. We do this together, right?" This life. This job. None of it meant anything without her by my side.

"We do, and we'll keep doing it together no matter what you choose." It wasn't much of an answer.

"And what should I choose?" I'd cut my wife out of too many decisions, deciding what was best for her. I wouldn't make this one without her input.

"What makes you happy," she said simply.

I took her hand and held it, feeling a tingle of electricity at her touch. "You. You make me happy."

"Well, you've got me no matter what," she promised and left it at that.

CHAPTER 29

CLARA

It wasn't the normal protocol to wait this long for the official royal birth announcement. One of Alexander's grandmothers had notoriously held out for nearly two months to spite her husband. But that had been decades ago, and with the advent of social media our decision to keep the details of William's birth private for nearly a month had speculation at an all-time high.

I did my best not to listen to any of it. It was enough, caring for a recuperating newborn and juggling a toddler. Buckingham suddenly felt as though it was bursting at the seams and empty at the same time.

It had been nearly a month since I'd spoken to Edward. I'd tried, but when Belle told me to respect his need for distance, I took her advice. At least he was speaking to her.

Three weeks ago, Sarah had been moved to Kensington Palace where Henry was keeping a close eye on her—along with a massive security team. She'd come to see the baby, failed to look me in the eye, and had left crying.

It felt like my family was falling apart at the same time that it felt stronger than ever.

Alexander strode out of the shower with a towel hanging off his hips just as I sat down to nurse William.

"You aren't ready," he said, looking me over.

It was true. I was stalling. I'd endured the media's questions before but this would be entirely different. Nothing could prepare me for facing them today after all that had happened. "You aren't either, but I'm not complaining."

I drank in the sight of his hard upper body, the muscles and scars carving across it, were a little too tempting. Alexander seemed to sense that my mind was in the gutter. Prowling toward me, he shook water from his hair, before bending down to kiss me.

"I believe the doctor said two more weeks." To us, waiting that long translated into a lifetime. Not that he hadn't found other ways to amuse himself. Once I'd finally convinced him that I wasn't going to shatter, we'd been engaging in other well-needed activities. "Unless you're ready for number three."

"Down, X." I pushed him away with my free hand. "Let's give this one a little more time."

"Like two weeks?" He smirked as he stood and allowed the towel to fall to the ground.

"That's playing dirty," I called to him as he sauntered to our closet, making a show of his shapely ass the whole way.

"I don't play any other way."

He was in a good mood considering the day's itinerary. It made me a little nervous. Then again, he'd had me home for weeks, neither of us interested in leaving. A new baby was a perfect excuse to stay in and we'd taken full advantage.

But although time had passed, we'd only just begun to heal. This time I knew the scars would never fade. We would carry them with us for the rest of our lives.

A few hours later the next stage of our lives was about to begin. We'd discussed what to say for hours, planned every word, but now that it was nearly here, I wasn't certain I could face it.

We'd call the press conference with a smaller number of reporters than normal, biasing our picks toward those that had been friendly to us in the past.

I smoothed the cotton wrap dress I'd chosen for the event, wondering if my stomach would ever be flat again. Exercise didn't feel like the highest priority for the moment, and Alexander certainly didn't have any complaints. I wondered again if I should have put my hair up. Then I remembered that it didn't really matter how I looked. People were interested in the baby.

Before we reached the White Room, a vaguely familiar older gentleman stepped into our path.

"If I might have a word, Your Majesty?" he said.

Alexander didn't seem shocked by the man's boldness. In fact, he appeared to recognize him. He took my arm and led us into a private room.

"Perhaps it would be best..." The stranger trailed away leaving me to fill in the blanks.

I was an uninvited guest, but before I could excuse myself and find Norris or Georgia—one of them would no doubt be lurking nearby—Alexander tightened his grip on my hand.

"I don't keep secrets from my wife. She knows about the Council."

I did my best to hide my shock and failed miserably. After hearing about the Council of Ghosts, I suppose I hadn't expected a man of flesh and blood to appear.

"Clara, this is Minister Clark," Alexander introduced us.

I ignored Clark's displeased look and smiled warmly at him—as warmly as a woman could smile at the man who might decide to assassinate her husband.

"There are unsettling rumors in Parliament," Clark said, bypassing continued pleasantries. "They say you plan to make an announcement today."

"We do," Alexander said serenely.

"And the nature of this announcement?"

"I suppose you'll find out. If you'll excuse us." Alexander directed us toward the corridor, but before we could step away, Clark clapped a hand on his shoulder.

"Think about what you're doing," he advised in a gruff voice. "You'll make enemies. This is a dangerous game you're playing."

Alexander shook free of him and considered this for a moment. "I'm done playing games."

I could barely keep up with his long strides as we made out way to the reporters. I felt the purpose blazing within him and suddenly my anxiety evaporated, replaced with pride.

This was the man I'd fallen in love with. He'd faced his

darkness. He'd embraced it. He'd chosen a path most men could never face. But Alexander didn't believe in accepting what fate handed him. He had rejected that lie a long time ago. Today, he was going to publicly show the world that he would not be intimidated.

He paused before we entered and pulled me close to him. Brushing a finger over my lips, he stared into my eyes, turning my core molten. "Are you ready?"

"Always," I breathed.

That's how it was with us. It would never change.

Alexander leaned down and covered my mouth with his, stealing my breath and replacing it with his own. For one wild moment, I forgot where we were and what we were about to do—and in that moment, everything made sense.

The sensation remained even when he finally drew away, as though he'd transfused me with his own confidence.

Norris stood on the edge of the room, scanning the crowd, always on the alert for danger. Eventually, I hoped he would forgive himself for what had happened. For now, I was glad he was here.

I hadn't been around this many strangers since Windsmoor, and it made my stomach flip. I felt my palm begin to sweat, but when I tried to pull it free, Alexander wouldn't let it go. The message was clear: we were in this together.

As soon as we took our place behind the podium, the questions began.

"Your Majesty, why the delay in introducing Prince William?"

"Your Majesty, are the rumors that the child nearly died true?"

"Your Majesty…"

"Your Majesty…"

"Your Majesty…"

They ran together, each a cutting reminder that our lives weren't our own.

Alexander held up his free hand and waited for the noise to die down. "Our son was born with a heart defect that required immediate surgery. We were aware of this and prepared. Out of consideration for his welfare and on medical advice, we've chosen to delay his introduction."

This announcement which ended a good deal of speculation propelled a new barrage of questions. Alexander bypassed them all. "We won't be sharing more details about William at this time. However, Clara and I have an announcement to make."

He looked to me. This was my part. I'd thought I could do it, but now that the time had come. I closed my eyes and willed a little more strength from him.

Alexander leaned over and whispered in my ear, "I'm here, poppet."

All around us cameras snapped photos of the moment. There was a reason why we were considered the most affectionate royal couple in history.

I squeezed Alexander's hand and forced myself to speak. "In May, a month before our son was due to be born, a group of people abducted me in an attempt to kidnap our child. Thanks to a courageous group of individuals—thanks to my family—I was recovered and William received the life-saving intervention he needed."

The room had fallen deadly silent. No one dared speak. It had been a gamble to tell them, but now that we had their attention, it was time to make our move.

I looked to Alexander, passing him the torch.

"This unprecedented action against the throne has forced us to establish new policies with the approval and aid of the Prime Minister to protect our family's well-being. This is no longer a matter of privacy. It is the matter of our very lives.

"Today the rogue organization known as MI-18 has been officially disavowed by the British government and placed at the top of Interpol's known terrorist organizations. Working with intelligence agencies throughout the world, we hope to bring these criminals to justice.

"I did not choose to be your King. It was a responsibility passed to me through birth. I'm proud of England—of what we stand for—so today I stand beside you not as a monarch but as a Brit. And I call upon you to stand up to those that would oppress and manipulate. We're a small nation but we are powerful. I'm proud to be your king and I will do everything in my power to protect my family and yours."

The silence stretched on for a moment, and when someone finally broke it, it wasn't with a question. I had no idea who the first person was to shout it, but the words rang loud and clear.

"Long live the King! Long live the Queen!"

Within seconds, the room was full of the chant. Alexander looked to me and smiled. We'd never be certain if we made the right choice. But there was one truth I would never doubt:

I never chose an easy life. I chose him.

Not ready for the story to end? Go to :
www.genevalee.com/vip

Want updates, exclusive bonus content, including the newsletter first book: **X** (Alexander's story)?
Become a VIP:
http://www.genevalee.com/vip

Love all things royal? Join my private reader group on facebook:
Geneva Lee's Loves

A glance, a kiss, and nothing would be the same...

Experience the beginning of the love affair.
A prince with a tragic past and dangerous secrets. An American woman who bows to no man. Their love story

shocks the world and threatens to destroy the Royal family from within.

Enter the seductive world of royalty in Command Me, the first volume in the bestselling Royals Saga, and discover why millions of readers all over the world have fallen in love with Alexander of Cambridge.

Free on all platforms.

READ COMMAND ME NOW!

To learn more about the Royals Saga, please visit: www.theroyalworld.online

CHAPTER 30

CLARA

It had been four months of waiting followed by gentle lovemaking, and I was going crazy. There were other changes: increased security around me and the children, which I no longer minded, along with increased media scrutiny, which I wouldn't have thought possible. Since our decision to announce most of the details of what had happened to me, I felt as though I was walking on eggshells. That combined with Alexander's careful handling of me left me feeling on edge. I needed to feel free, and there was only one way to do that safely—in his arms. Or, more accurately, tied up in his bed.

I laid in bed, stewing over the issue, Alexander snoring softly beside me, until a tiny cry rose from the bassinet at the foot of the bed. My husband sat up instantly, trained to respond to the sound of our son at all hours, but I was already up and gather William into my arms.

Alexander's gaze followed me as I went through the morning routine he usually handled. If I turned I would either see annoyance or lust written across his dark features.

"I was already awake, X," I told him as I checked William's diaper and wrapped him into a blanket.

"You do more than enough. I can change the nappies." He hated when I usurped his duties. Considering my duties consisted mostly of feeding and cuddling the baby while attending Elizabeth's tea parties, I was certain I was getting the better end of the deal.

Normally, I would carry the baby to a chair and nurse him, but this morning, I brought him into bed with us. Alexander was propped, bleary-eyed, against the headboard, a sheet concealing nothing but his groin. My eyes raked over the stack of muscles that narrowed downward in invitation. It was a bit unfair really. My own body was softer than ever, my stomach still a bit too full following birth, my hips somehow wider. Nothing about him had changed, except that he might have gotten sexier.

"What was that?" he asked, scooping up a pillow blocking him from reaching us and depositing it on the floor.

"Nothing," I lied.

"I distinctly saw a frown when you looked at me." He glanced down, running his palm over the ridges of his abs like he expected to find something wrong. "Don't like you what you see, poppet?"

"That's not it." I liked it a little too much, regardless of how I felt about myself at the moment. I liked it enough that I was ready to bind my own wrists and offer myself to him like a sacrifice—if only I had any hope he'd take it.

"I could order you to tell me." His mouth twisted into a crooked grin. He knew he wouldn't have to go to that extreme, but he loved to rile me up.

"That doesn't work on me, X." I shifted the baby, who was already blinking his eyes with sleepy happiness. This was all he knew—his mother and father and safety and warmth. How could I ask for more than that after everything? How could I want more?

"Then tell me because I love you," he murmured, trailing a finger down my shoulder as he drank in the sight of his wife and child.

"You're so..." I let my eyes do the talking, running them up and down him appreciatively. "But it's been four months and look at me."

"Trust me, I am." There was no mistaking the desire running like a current through his words. It was another reason I felt terrible bringing it up. Our sex life hadn't exactly suffered since we'd been given the all clear to resume normal activities. The issue was that we hadn't resumed normal activities.

Instead, Alexander had placed me on a pedestal, treating me as though I was a priceless object and handling me accordingly. We'd been down this road before but I'd thought we were past it. Now it felt like a button had been pushed sending us back to the start.

And there was only one way to fix it.

"Then why won't you fuck me?" I asked, feeling a slight wave of guilt that I was bringing this up with our son in my arms.

Alexander blinked, his finger halting in place over a

freckle. "I believe I have, poppet. Last night. The night before."

"That's not what I mean," I said pointedly. "Making love every night isn't the same as...other things."

Alexander drew back, pain flashing across his face but he refused to let it settle there. Still, it lingered in his eyes. "I wasn't sure after what had happened..."

I felt like an idiot. Of course, this wasn't about me being unbreakable. It was about the kidnapping, a memory both of us were struggling to overcome.

"They didn't do anything like that," I said softly. We'd been over the details numerous times officially and privately, but I suspected Alexander thought I was protecting him from certain facts.

"Still, it was against your will and..." he trailed off, looking torn. The truth was that part of my own need stemmed from his. His touch had been leashed the last few months. At first, that was fine given the changes my body had experienced. Now? I wanted all of him.

"Alexander, I'm living in a fishbowl," I said quietly, continuing on before he could become defensive, "and we both know it's for the best. But there's only one place where I can be safe and completely free—and there's only one place where you can have the control you need."

His eyes grew darker, hooding slightly, at the suggestion of my words, but he shook himself free of it. "I don't want to hurt you."

"You won't." There was so much changing in our lives but that fact wouldn't. Nothing bad would ever happen to me while he was in control of my body.

Alexander didn't speak for a moment, but his tongue darted over his lower lip as though he was considering the possibilities. That was a very good sign. Then he said the words I was longing to hear. "Tonight."

THE REST OF MY DAY WAS SPENT RESTLESSLY attending to daily life as my anticipation grew to a fever pitch. In so many ways Alexander and I had been more connected than ever, especially since we'd made the decision to retain our titles. But there had been something missing—a bond we shared that was so intimate it felt like a part of me. Knowing I was on the verge of rekindling that connection left me staring at the clock.

There were a few distractions. William chose that afternoon to roll over the first time, and I sat impatiently camera trained on him waiting for him to do it again.

"Clever boy," I coaxed earning a happy gurgle but little movement. Instead of rolling, he grabbed his toes and tried to stick them in his mouth.

There'd been some concern that he would experience delayed milestones following his surgery, but he continued to prove the doctors wrong. This was the most recent proof that he was strong and healthy. I was about to give up when Elizabeth toddled into the nursery with her Aunt Belle at her heels. Their entrance sparked Wills' curiosity and he rolled to see who had intruded upon his domain.

"Oh!" Belle clapped, earning a studious glance from Elizabeth who followed suit. My daughter was fairly certain my best friend hung the moon.

She'd been helping out the last few months while William recovered and we adjusted to our new life as a family of four. It had been a joint decision to dismiss Nanny Penny and not hire anyone else to care for the children. Knowing that MI-18's agenda hinged on them made it difficult to trust anyone. But caring for an active toddler and a newborn with medical needs had made us more reliant than ever on our friends, even Georgia had stepped up and helped us out on a few occasions.

But looking up from my son to Belle's rounded face and belly, I knew that time was coming to a close. She was already a week overdue with her daughter.

"I wasn't sure we'd see you today," I admitted. Every night I expected to get the phone call that she was finally in labor.

"I'm going to serve the baby a vacate notice." She trudged across the room and lowered herself with a grateful sigh into the glider. "I feel as big as a house."

"You look gorgeous." I wasn't saying this simply to boost her spirits. Pregnancy suited Belle. Other than fuller cheeks and a round stomach, she looked exactly the same with an added glow that radiated off her.

She patted her stomach. "I'm just ready to meet this little one."

I understood where she was coming from. Rewatching the video of William's accomplishment, I sighed and sent it to his father.

"You should send it to him," Belle said softly.

"Alexander hates missing this stuff." But we both knew it wasn't my husband I was thinking of right now.

"You know what I meant," she said with meaning. I always felt Edward's absence most acutely when I was with Belle. Despite meeting him years after her, I'd come to expect all three of us to be together whenever possible. I hadn't seen Edward for nearly four months.

"Have you spoken with him?" I asked. Edward seemed to be avoiding all of us since his husband's death, but Alexander and I the most.

"For a few minutes," she said. "He called to tell me he was going to Italy."

"Italy?" I raised an eyebrow. Edward had bounced from country to country for weeks.

"He said he's eating all the pasta and getting fat." Belle smiled sadly.

"He's never going to forgive me," I murmured. I was the reason David was dead—the reason he hadn't been given a chance to say goodbye.

"It's not you that he has to forgive," Belle reminded me. "He needs time to process what David did and what..."

She trailed away, but I knew what she was thinking: *what Alexander did.* I knew that my husband had acted instinctively and I knew he blamed himself for Edward's self-appointed exile.

But if I'd been the one with the gun, I'm not certain I wouldn't have done the same.

"He'll come back," Belle said firmly, leaving no room for doubt. I felt it anyway. "Send him the video."

I considered for a moment before I took her advice. I knew better than to expect a response, but maybe what Edward needed—maybe the only thing I could give him—

was a reminder that his family was still here when he was ready to return home.

The bassinet had been moved across the bedroom when I came in to nurse William to sleep that evening. Elizabeth was already asleep in her bed. Dinner had been a series of shy smiles and double entendre. My heart jumped a little at the sight. This was really happening. Alexander hadn't appeared since he'd gone to meet with Norris for one final briefing after we'd eaten together as a family, and he didn't arrive until William was nursing lazily, already a little milk drunk.

I'd hoped to have a few minutes to change into something sexier than the robe I'd thrown on earlier, but that didn't seem to matter to Alexander. He loomed in the doorway, watching me, with an intensity that melted my core. He stayed like that for a few minutes, not speaking, until he finally made his way to us, lifted our sleeping son from my arms and carried him to the bassinet. I stole the opportunity to duck into the bathroom and check myself in the mirror. Playing for a moment with the robe—letting it hang open, allowing it to fall off my shoulder—I finally gave up and cinched it tightly before returning to the bedroom.

Alexander was standing outside the door, stripped down to his slacks, belt in hand. I hesitated for a moment, taken back by the powerful surge of emotions I felt. Every part of me wanted to kneel before him and wait for his commands. Every part of me wanted to go to him and kiss him, eager to feel his hands on me. Every part of me trembled with anticipation over what came next.

"You don't need that," he spoke in a low voice that raked over my skin and send goosebumps rippling across my body. How could he turn me on with simple words alone?

I unfastened it and let the robe puddle to the floor. Alexander's gaze skimmed over me slowly, erasing any doubt I'd felt about my changed body and replacing it with the surety of his desire.

"Come to me," he ordered. I took a step toward him and he shook his head, pointing down.

I knew what he wanted and I did it without hesitation, dropping one knee at a time and lowering myself to crawl the few feet to him. My breasts swayed, heavy and fully, as I moved toward his feet. When I reached them, I leaned down and kissed the toe of his shoe without thinking.

Alexander sucked in a breath. "Pretty poppet knows her place and likes it, does she?"

I looked up to him, love pouring through me, and nodded. Yes, I loved this. I loved him.

I loved handing him control and holding on as he took me where I wasn't brave enough to go alone. That was the magic of it—the truth. There was freedom in restraint.

"You feared this once." He brushed the tip of the belt over my cheek. "Now you don't even blink. Why?"

"Because I love you. Because I trust you." My answer was simple. So many things had changed between us. The roots of our love grew so deeply no storm could shake us.

Alexander's nostrils flared and I knew he wanted to use

the belt on me. I knew he was imagining the red stripes it would form along my backside, but his head swiveled to the bassinet. "Someday."

I would count the minutes until then. For now, though, I felt bold—or perhaps, I knew that egging him on would spur him to take control more quickly. Sitting back on my heels, I brushed my lips swiftly over the bulge in his bands.

"Someone wants to test me," he growled. "I promise there are other ways I can mark your body."

The memory of his teeth flashed through my mind and my muscles clenched.

"You want this." He stroked his cock through the fabric as he walked a circle around me. "Maybe I'll make you wait. Maybe I'll see all the ways I can make you come without it."

I felt my lower lip slip out in answer to his threat. I didn't want to wait. I wanted him to shove his cock in my mouth. I wanted him to throw me onto the bed and plunge inside me. In short, I wanted him.

"You look displeased," he noted. "Might I suggest you behave?"

I nodded in agreement.

"Good. Crawl to the bed, poppet." He pointed to the foot of it.

I did as I was told, feeling his eyes lingering as my knees and palms slapped across the floor. He made me wait another few minutes before he finally strolled over and dropped into a crouch beside me.

"Now I know how hard it is to keep all those beautiful little cries to yourself," he murmured, tracing the curve of my neck with his finger, "but we have company, so I'm afraid you have to. Can you do that?"

I bit my lip, knowing there was no way to make that promise. When we were making love, he smothered the noise with his mouth. I got the impression that this evening his mouth would be otherwise occupied.

"I didn't think so." He looked pleased about this. "Kneel at the edge of the bed."

I moved onto my knees, folding over the mattress, breathless with excitement. Alexander's hands swept my hair over my shoulders and slowly began to braid it. When he was finished, he withdrew something from his pocket and took a seat next to me.

"Open your mouth." I parted my lips obediently and felt a soft but firm ball press between them.

"This will help you stay quiet, poppet," he explained as he buckled the gag around my head. When he was finished he brushed a finger down my cheek. Alexander's eyes were on fire and I was burning in the flame. I was ready for what-ever he had in store for me.

Picking up the belt he'd laid across the mattress, he directed me to hold out my arms. I crossed my wrists expec-tantly, feeling my core tighten each time he coiled the strap around them. When he'd pulled the buckle firmly into place, I felt something silky press into my palm.

"Hold onto that," he said. "You won't be able to speak with this in place. If it becomes too much, drop the hand-kerchief and I'll stop."

Even as he relinquished himself to the primitive side he tried to cage, he always thought of me. I clutched the silk square tightly, hoping I didn't accidentally send him the wrong idea. I had no plans of letting it go this evening regardless of his concerns.

Alexander moved behind me, leaving me folded over the bed, bound and gagged, and I wondered what delicious surprise came next. Then I heard the metallic clang of the spreader bar hit the rug. His hands worked quickly, securing my ankles, until I was spread before him.

"I know what you want," he murmured as he dragged a palm down my back before cupping my ass. "But I know what you need. I want you soft and ready and wet, so I think we need to start here."

His hand slipped between my legs before he eased a finger inside me and began to leisurely pump, another joined it as his thumb stroked across my swollen clit, and I found my teeth sinking into the ball gag.

"This isn't foreplay, poppet," he warned me. "I expect you to come and quickly. Let go."

It was natural to want to hold out—to ride the intensity building inside me longer before crashing into pleasure. But I knew Alexander, and I knew there was more pleasure waiting for me as the evening continued. I relaxed into his touch, allowing his fingers to work me toward a rapid build up of tension. Then he shifted his movements, curling his fingers until my whole body spasmed and I came against his hand with a startling gush.

"That was so fucking hot." He leaned forward and kissed me, whispering in my ear, "You're going to be dripping all night—ready for my cock whenever I finally decide to give it to you."

The gag stole my answering whimper but I squirmed closer, pushing my ass against him like I was sending an engraved invitation. Alexander loosed a low laugh and withdrew his hand, leaving me feeling hollow and desperate for more.

"Now that you're relaxed, let's see what we can do to set you free." He stood and left me there, bound and naked, and moved across the room. When he returned, he had a velvet hanger in his hands. My eyes widened as I took it in and he laughed again. "Trust me. If you don't..."

He glanced toward my hands where I still clutched the silk handkerchief.

"This won't leave the marks you enjoy, poppet, but I'm rather enjoying how pristine your ass looks like this and it is much quieter." He rounded me, until I could no longer see him. "Just think. I could take this anytime, anyplace and spank you soundly without anyone hearing. Isn't that a lovely thought?"

I moaned into the gag, hoping that was true. His palm circled my bottom lovingly before disappearing. A moment later, a soft thwap spread warmth across both cheeks. It was gentle and hard at the same time. Without the accompanying smacks I'd grown accustomed to, each strike was a lovely surprise. It took effort to not tense my body in anticipation. I willed myself to relax and allow the spanking to come as he decided.

"Very good," he said encouragingly. "I can feel you inviting them. They're turning your bottom a lovely shade of pink."

I could feel the heat and knew it was true. It was

different than the other spankings I'd submitted to, but somehow even more erotic for the quiet intimacy of it. Not that I would say no the next time Alexander spread me over his lap, but it was more enjoyable than I'd expected.

I lost track of the time, my limbs softening as he liberated my body until I was sagging against the bed. I barely noticed when he stopped until his palm slid against my sex.

"Still ready for me," he said gruffly. "I can't decide how I want you, though. This is such a lovely picture. I'd like to fuck you like this, but I think..."

I didn't care what he did. I'd allow any of it. I was mildly surprised when I felt the belt on my wrists loosen and slip away. Alexander rubbed the indents it left in my skin, but I heard the shuddering, laboured quality of his breathing. He loved the small marks—the reminders that my body had been given to him utterly. I wanted to tell him to put the strap back. I wasn't ready to be free yet. But the gag was still in place.

He guided me to my feet carefully, not removing the bar that kept my legs spread open. "Just one moment."

His hand flattened, pushing me to the mattress and without warning, his cock thrust inside me. I cried out, but it was muffled. I would never get enough of this. I would never stop wanting him.

"It's just as beautiful as I imagined." He ran his hands over my warm bottom as he withdrew inch by inch until the silky head of his bobbed along my swollen seam. I wiggled against it, trying to recapture him but he held me in place. "Such a hungry little cunt. I only wanted to see how pretty you'd look full of my cock with a bright red ass. Now I'm ready. Are you ready?"

I released a frustrated sob and nodded. Alexander bent and gathered me into his arms, kissing my shoulders as he maneuvered my body around and lifted me onto the bed. Reaching down he lifted my legs over his shoulders until the bar was spread against his broad shoulders. "Your ass is pretty, but I want to watch you come."

I nodded, trying to spread my legs wider, as though he needed more of an invitation, only to be met by resistance.

"Just a minute." He guided his cock along my slick seam without breaching me. "I like watching you squirm and actually, I've been neglecting these."

His free hand snaked up to my left breast, cupping it before closing over my nipple and beginning to massage, earning him a gentle trickle of milk. I stared as he lifted the fingers to his mouth and licked it off. "I love every bit of you," he reminded me, "especially how you taste."

My head fell back, unable to take another moment of teasing. He must have sensed this because I felt his cock push slowly inside me. To say it felt good was an insult to the idea of understatements. He'd lit me on fire and now he was stroking the flame. I wanted to rock against him, but thanks to the careful positioning of the bar, he was in complete control of each thrust. He knew it and took his time.

"I love you," he said quietly before he unleashed himself, driving into me until I shattered against him, coming again when I felt his release lashing inside me.

When he finally withdrew, his finger whispered across

my aching sex with satisfaction. It took a few minutes to undo the gag and bar, but then I was in his arms where he held me close, whispering praise and love. I felt like I was floating and he was my anchor.

That's what love was, after all. Freedom and codependence. Beauty and pain. Joy and sorrow. Love encompassed it all. Love made us strong by bringing us to our knees. Love taught us not to look for answers but rather truth—and Alexander was the only truth I ever needed to know.

ACKNOWLEDGMENTS

This was the hardest book I've ever written, physically and mentally. Life handed me a huge responsibility in the midst of working on this, and as I sit here, shaking, trembling, and wondering how the hell, I got through, you're the person I want to thank.

The one who's loved these books, rooted for these characters, and kept me going.

I'm blessed to have a wonderful team behind me that knows exactly why I'm keeping these nods short and sweet. I couldn't do this without you—any of it.

Thank you. Always.

www.ingramcontent.com/pod-product-compliance
Lightning Source LLC
Chambersburg PA
CBHW050824190726
48286CB00007B/1982